First published 2000 by Diva Books
an imprint of Millivres Limited
part of the Millivres Prowler Group
116-134 Bayham Street, London NW1 0BA

A catalogue record for this book is available from the British Library

ISBN 1 873741 43 X

Printed and bound by WS Bookwell, Finland 2000

THE COMEDIENNE

VG LEE

VG Lee is a founder member of All Mouth No Trousers literary cabaret group, in which *The Comedienne* first gained a cult following as 'The Joanie Stories'. Val's poems and short stories have appeared in various magazines and anthologies and been made into two BBC short films. Born in Birmingham, she now lives and writes in Hackney, London.

To M.V.

PART ONE

TAPE 1

Joan: I'm sorry. My memory's lousy. As mum said on several occasions... oh god, what was it she said?

Q: Your mother featured quite strongly in your stage act; would you say she's been the most stable relationship in your life?

Joan: Mothers often are, aren't they? I mean, lovers come and go. You can hang on to a cat longer than you can a lover. (Pause) I hung on to my cat longer than I ever kept a lover.

Q: Is she still alive?

Joan: Oh yes, Edith's fifteen, would you believe? She can still be quite kittenish.

Q: No, I meant your mother.

Joan: She died recently.

Q: I'm sorry.

Joan: Funnily enough, so was I.

Q: Going back to lovers; how often have you been in love?

Joan: Let's see: Mrs. Bryant in Biology Class, Sandy, Steff, Susan... I had a run on the 's' names. Jennifer from Homebase, Monica Stewart the form prefect.

Q: Truly, madly, deeply in love?

Joan: (Pause) Once.

ONE
1980
Once upon a time there was Susan...

I'm mad about Susan, which mum reckons is ridiculous at twenty-six, and can't I just like her as she likes, say, Nurse Duggan? "Hello again. Not too bad, and you? Did the little Duggans behave themselves at the weekend?" That sort of stuff. Why must I be mad about someone to the extent of rustling our net curtains every weekday morning, just to see Susan pass by our house, in her silver-grey Cortina, one hand on the wheel, the other sliding in a country and western cassette?

"It's not as if she ever looks up at you or bibs her horn. You make yourself pathetic," mum said, on her second cup of tea, and showing no sign of getting up and going into the bathroom.

"She can't look up at me and put in a cassette at the same time."

"She could put the cassette in when she gets in the car. She's using you because you're convenient. Very nice – a ladyfriend on her doorstep."

"I'm not her ladyfriend, I'm her partner."

"Don't try being modern, madam. That one will have women in Coventry. Women in frocks."

"Mum, are you getting up and having a wash this morning, or what?"

"Why can't I stay put?" she whined, "I'm back in bed for a nap at two, asleep again by nine. Where's the point?"

I'm coming around to her way of thinking. I mean, it's like her hair – she doesn't do much to get it that dirty any more, which is fortunate because she's developed an aversion to water. On several occasions I've considered asking Nurse Duggan's advice, but it's impossible getting her to myself. Mum's hearing is exceptional. She has a sixth sense if she's the subject under discussion. Even when I walk Nurse D to the gate, mum's at the window, lip-reading.

One evening last summer, Susan and I were halfway down the garden exchanging a few loving intimacies while pretending to discuss what to do about the outbreak of black spot on the 'Sarabande' red rose she'd bought me for Easter; I looked back towards the house and there was mum staring eerily at us through a glass of water. An hour later, when Susan had gone home and I was puzzling over a cryptic crossword, mum suddenly piped up from her armchair: "How can you say 'I love you' to a woman you've never even been shopping with?"

"I don't go shopping with you mum, yet I retain a certain affection for you."

"Very austere. You're not like that with Lady May."

"Her name's Susan. Could you hear us from the kitchen?"

"I didn't need to. I was watching the silly expression on your face."

I could say that it wasn't that easy growing up as a lesbian in Birmingham, but on the other hand, for me, it wasn't that hard either, because I was always more concerned about mum, over and above the crushes I periodically had on teachers or friends. It was like forever running after a bus (the bus being mum), that might just stop and let me get my foot on the platform if the traffic lights changed. While running, I might notice someone eating chips. (For 'chips' read my sexual preference.) There was never time to worry about wanting the chips. I'd think as I ran past, "Yum, yum, they smell/look delicious," but chips were for when I had time to pause for a breather and mum didn't allow pauses for breathers. Not when I was a child, nor for much of my teens.

I was born in 1953. She was forty-four. We lived in a Victorian terraced house in Smallheath in the days when a Victorian terrace was the last thing anyone wanted to live in. It was cold and damp and one side was held up by three metal girders because the house next door had been flattened by a bomb. Mum rather liked this. She said a) it meant we were end-mid-terrace, b) the gap between the houses afforded us a measure of privacy, and c) we had our own link to a very important chunk of British history. I liked the fact that we had a 'cut-through' into Raglan Street which meant I could knock a good four minutes off my journey to school plus avoiding having to see or speak to our immediate neighbours. I hated our neighbours and was quite satisfied for them to hate me. I was 'that odd little girl of Mrs Littler's' who grew up to be 'that gawky great woman with the queer ideas and queerer friends'. Most of this hatred stuff was in my head. It was what I imagined they said, brawny arms folded, headscarfed heads nodding. I rarely tested out a confrontation. As a rule I kept myself to myself; I could be set back for a whole day if someone surprised a 'Good morning' out of me.

We never had a Mr Littler. I wasn't a child that ran in from school, tears pouring down my face, to bawl, "Why haven't I got a daddy like all the other children, marmee?"

No. I brooded well into my teens, waiting for mum to broach the subject. I watched, noted, kept my ears to the ground. Nothing. Mrs Botolph and Mrs Scott – mum's 'only two, true friends' and my sworn enemies – sometimes mentioned 'the father' but they were always shushed by mum and ushered into the front room where they murmured behind a closed and curtained (to keep out the draught) door.

Sixteen, a sunny afternoon (I often take the bull by the horns on sunny afternoons), I came in from school, dumped my briefcase down on the hearth rug with a thump to get mum's attention. She was off work with a cold and was hunched over a large piece of navy knitting. I said loudly, "Just who was my dad, mum? People often enquire at school and I would like to stop looking enigmatic."

"People?" she said, raising her eyebrows and giving the

knitting an amused look.

"People. Friends. Well, I'd like to know. Obviously I am interested in who my dad was."

Mum laid the knitting down on her lap and took off her glasses. She began to clean them on what was left of her ounce of four-ply, which made me think she might be about to cry for the first time ever, but no, she was only cleaning her glasses.

She said, "Joan, 'Soldiers are citizens of death's grey land,'" which wasn't the reply I'd been waiting for.

I was at the surly stage in my development which lasted for the next two decades. My fists were knocking the shape out of my blazer pockets and I was chewing a wad of Kleenex tissue because I couldn't afford chewing gum. I said, "So what?"

"Well, so use your bloody loaf," she answered. She often used minor swear words in those days – 'bloody', 'bugger' and 's.o.b.' As she grew older she shifted to 'rapscallion', 'nincompoop' and 'ignoramus', which I imagine had a lot to do with her eventual obsession with crossword puzzles, which is an irrelevant piece of information but quite nice to set the scene.

I said, "Are you saying that dad is, was, a dead soldier?"

She started knitting again. "I am merely quoting from a poem. Put kettle on."

Over tea I had a bit of a think. Tea was never very special in our house, usually what mum called, 'the world and his wife on toast,' and afterwards I made her recite the poem. She knew it by heart which surprised me. I asked her if she knew any other poems and she said, "Maybe," but she never repeated any more. I wrote this one down. I've still got it. Somewhere in there is my father.

DREAMERS
by Siegfried Sassoon

Soldiers are citizens of death's grey land,
Drawing no dividend from time's to-morrows.
In the great hour of destiny they stand,
Each with his feuds, and jealousies, and sorrows.
Soldiers are sworn to action; they must win
Some flaming, fatal climax with their lives.
Soldiers are dreamers; when the guns begin,
They think of firelit homes, clean beds, and wives.

I see them in foul dug-outs, gnawed by rats,
And in the ruined trenches, lashed with rain,
Dreaming of things they did with balls and bats,
And mocked by hopeless longing to regain
Bank-holidays, and picture shows, and spats,
And going to the office in the train.

"And you can't give me any more information than that?" I persisted, following ketchup around the rim of my plate with a slice of staleish bread.

"I don't want to."

"Is it too painful?"

"I don't want to talk about it."

"Then I must assume it is too painful and that tragedy lurks behind your reluctant exterior," I said pompously.

She put the tea cosy on my head and patted it down over my ears. I left it on for the rest of the evening. It felt warm and soft and our house was cold and inhospitable for three quarters of the year. Even later, when I went to bed, I was reluctant to take it off. I'd intended to fall asleep thinking about my mystery father but instead nodded off over leaving school and marketing tea cosies for those with habitually cold ears and feet.

I've little social life these days apart from tea with mum and Nurse Duggan; and Susan of course. We have to be careful both living in the same road. Mum says her name has been a byword for respectability in this area for nearly sixty years and she'll have no shenanigans besmirching it now that she's on her last knockings.

Of course she's not on her last knockings. She'll twitch, gasp and complain for years yet. I try to see her as a courageous old rogue. "Wrong," Susan says.

How does mum see me? She doesn't always appreciate the sacrifices I've made on her behalf. Her version is that my birth made an old woman of her, ruined her taste for gin and pig's liver which up until her pregnancy had been the only little luxuries she could afford in a cruel world.

"And you believe her?" Susan again. "What about the pots and pills and smellies? What about those hats trimmed with endangered species on top of her wardrobe? What about the diamanté suede sandals in the trunk under her bed? Don't feel guilty, Joan, she's had her fun, it's you that's done without, believe you me."

Susan knows a lot about human nature, being a social worker and getting exceedingly good money. It's surprising how adversely she reacts to mum. It's surprising how mum reacts against Susan. It would be nice to imagine myself as the high point of a jealous isosceles triangle, but the fact is, neither likes the other.

I hadn't always lived in Birmingham with mum. When I was twenty-one I got out, went down to London. Found a job in a store in the West End. For a year or two I was my own woman, mum only a busy little memory at the back of my head that I was able to ignore for weeks at a time. Then one Friday lunchtime, there was a fire drill at work. Shop and office staff all assembled in Hanover Square at the back of Oxford Street. We answered our names and were checked off the staff list. The sky was a hard brilliant blue.

It looked miles away. It probably is miles away, only at home, in Smallheath, it seemed closer and softer. Like a light blue blanket, or would a light blue cotton sheet give a better idea? Imagine something light and blue that feels soft and warm on a cold face. I thought of our garden and the two plane trees at the bottom, which fortunately threw shadow all day into the garden behind ours. I worked it out. While everyone discussed where was best for a cup of tea, us all being used to sitting in the canteen however pleasant the weather, I could be in mum's kitchen by five. It would still be hot and she could cook me fish fingers and chips. I'd ring my flatmate in the evening and explain, catch a train back to London very early on Monday morning.

I went in search of my immediate boss, my face only slightly contorted in pain. I didn't want to overdo things. I found her applying magenta lipstick and squinting into an Estée Lauder powder compact.

"Yes Joan," she said without turning around and without a word of introduction from me.

"I'm terribly sorry, Mrs Spring, but I think my period's started."

"You think?" She blotted her lips distractedly. Mrs Spring came from mum's school of conversation which had raised interrogation to an art form.

"I know."

"What do you want me to do about it?"

"Nothing. I just wanted to tell you. I think I'll have to go home."

She closed her compact. Slipped it and her lipstick into her immaculate Louis Vuitton handbag and gave me her full attention.

"What you mean, Joan, is it's a lovely sunny day, and you'd rather be at home beginning your weekend early."

I winced with pain and gave a small gasp.

"No Mrs Spring, I really do have a very painful period. I am considering going to the doctor's to see about a new tablet on the market that's supposed to moderate the flow of blood..."

She held up her hand in distaste. "Spare me, Joan, please. Go home. I'm not about to hold you here by force."

I was off, hobbling away into the crowd before remembering I shouldn't be hobbling, I should be crouching and gasping.

By ten to four I was walking down our deserted road. It was too early for the homeward trickle. I thought how much I loved our particular street, what a good thing that the council had let us buy our house instead of enforcing the demolition order, and how fortunate that of all our neighbours, horrible bunch that they were, not one had stone cladded. Every house retained the crumbly grey brickwork that turned to silver blue in winter but at that moment glowed a warm amber. I felt like singing. Composing a tune to 'I love Smallheath, but I'd die of boredom if I stayed'.

I hummed my way up our path, into the hall; I could hear the radio on in the kitchen.

"Mum, guess who?" I shouted and barged in. I blinked. It wasn't our kitchen. Our kitchen was often messy, but this was a tip. The only object immediately familiar was mum. She was sitting at the cluttered kitchen table eating a large, untidy sandwich. Her mouth was open in expectation, which changed to surprise at seeing me gawping in the doorway. Her sandwich hovered, poised for that first bite.

I said, "Why are you wearing pink rubber gloves?"

She bit into the sandwich, said, "None of your business," with her mouth full.

The joints of her hands weren't working; rheumatoid arthritis. I hadn't noticed, her fingers were like claws, her grip as weak as a child's. The rubber gloves were her way of dealing with opening jars, turning taps on and off, gripping the banisters. She'd become dependent on them, putting them on when she went into the bathroom each morning, taking them off when she went to bed at night. When I peeled the gloves off, I saw they'd caused a rash between each of her bent fingers. I probably decided to move back then and there. It took me another three months to act on that decision.

I receive a small allowance from the State for looking after mum. Nurse Duggan and Susan tell me I could claim more but I'm not complaining. I've tried to explain to Susan that I shouldn't need payment to look after my own mother, but Susan says, "Correction, Joanie love, you shouldn't need payment to look after most mothers, yours is the exception. I wouldn't do it for all the tea in China."

That's a phrase Sue shares with mum. She doesn't know it and I'd never point it out. They both have their sayings, small idiosyncrasies of speech. Susan puts mum's down to early senility, which it isn't; mum says Susan's crude and foul-mouthed, which she is sometimes, but I don't mind. In fact I find it attractive. That makes mum shudder and say, "I don't know how you can, Joan." By this, she means our sleeping arrangements.

***

Within a few months of coming back home to look after mum, my fashion sense went downhill. I bought cheap jogging suits in the market, then, influenced by Nurse D, who had particular ideas on how spinster daughters should look, I added several drab coloured 'button-throughs', or what mum called 'pinafore dresses' to my wardrobe. It was as if my short and sweet worldly life was over – like entering holy orders, suddenly it seemed necessary to be suitably attired. I walked with eyes downcast, my head bowed to my fate. That was when Susan first noticed me.

To get to the local shops, I had to pass her house. She said that every Saturday morning she'd watch me droop past down the hill pulling my empty Black Watch tartan trolley. She thought what a crying waste of a face and figure like mine. Which was very flattering. Years later, I did wonder why, if I had such a striking face and figure, did she never hang about to catch me drooping back up the hill with a full trolley?

I was twenty-three when Susan turned my life around. I kept the trolley. It was very useful as Susan never offered to drive me to the shops. She said she didn't want to mix our very different lifestyles and a measure of space between two people kept a relationship fresh.

I caught up again. Trainers, jeans and tight jumpers; T-shirts and halter-neck tops in summer. For special evenings at Susan's, when she cooked with all the trimmings, I bought a pair of black leather trousers that I tucked into Cuban heeled cowboy boots with turquoise and silver tooling snaking up their sides.

Mum tried them on and said, "If you want to make a laughing stock of yourself in the road and cripple your feet into the bargain, could you please do it after dark?"

Although mum is light, she's an awkward shape, difficult to get to grips with. For months she can manage on her own, get up, get herself dressed, then suddenly the simplest movement becomes unbearably painful. It's like trying to manipulate a bundle of badly tied twigs – bits keep falling out of my arms. Usually I get her down for breakfast by nine-thirty. She has toast, marmalade and two cups of tea while she reads the newspaper headlines, or starts on an article in a magazine.

"This chap got melanoma in the ankle just by playing golf," she said one morning.

"Really?"

"Dead in a year."

"How was that then?"

"Hang on." She went back to the newspaper.

I was washing up her tea things from the night before and daydreaming that it was five-thirty and I was preparing dinner for Susan to come in to at seven. In my dream, I stood in Susan's stainless steel kitchen with its set of painted wood-handled knives and matching enamel saucepans. In my daydream, mum wasn't dead, only conveniently elsewhere. In a pleasant residential home of her choice. Better still, she'd upped sticks to live with my cousin in the Cotswolds – which was more than highly unlikely.

"Where does Susan go on a Sunday and Tuesday evening?" she asked, folding the paper over at the sports pages.

I paused in my humming of 'Secret Love'. It was so like mum to trickle acid across my happiest thoughts.

"She has friends," I replied cautiously. "What about your golf fatality?"

"I told you, dead within the year. Founded a leprosy clinic and then kaput. You never mention her friends."

"We lead separate lives. I don't mention you if I can help it."

"That's different," she persisted. "Have you ever met any of her friends?"

"Don't start making trouble."

"I only want your happiness," she said in the wheedling, insincere voice she uses to annoy me.

"I am happy, thank you. Extremely happy."

Of course, being mum, she'd touched on the very spot that troubled me. Why hadn't I been introduced to Susan's friends? Quite early on in our relationship, I'd asked her that very question as I sat curled next to her on her four-person leather sofa.

"I want you all to myself, Joanie." She'd squeezed me tighter against her crisp cotton shirt, which had satisfied me perfectly at the time. Her words made me feel delicate and precious, which I'd never felt before and to be honest only ever felt when I was with her.

At that time, I hadn't really wanted to meet her friends. I was nervous of the comparison between them and me. I was only just out of my 'button-throughs' and what could I offer for conversation? They wouldn't want to hear about mum and her tantrums, shopping and my skills with invalid diets and how to enforce a bed bath.

Three nights a week I had Susan all to myself. I settled mum down with the television and a stack of fresh reading. Two nights we stayed in our own houses and two nights, Sunday and Tuesday, I stayed in my own house, and Susan saw her friends. I was never included. I'd tried light-hearted, disinterested questioning and received only the sketchiest of replies.

"Clare and Paddy made their spaghetti, we played Monopoly until late, a gang of us met up in the wine bar after work."

And descriptions. Clare and Paddy were 'really nice women', another pair were 'a lot of laughs' and a woman called Jo was 'big trouble' and so on.

"What's Clare and Paddy's flat like then?" I'd asked.

"Muted colours."

"In what way a lot of laughs?"

"They just make me die, that's all. You can't explain comedy, lovey."

"And big trouble Jo?"

"Don't ask me. I wouldn't know where to start."

Because of their mutual animosity, mum and Susan rarely met. Mum was the nastier of the two as she had more time on her hands to dwell on things. She picked on everything I liked or admired about Susan, from her shiny, chestnut hair, kept shortish but long enough to sweep behind her ears, to her stone-coloured jeans and leather jacket.

"Tommy Steele in the Fifties. She only needs a guitar. It's disgusting," mum said.

"What is?"

"Going with a woman. I never did, not once in all my years at the office."

"You went with a man at your office party. I remember you waking me up and saying you might be pregnant."

"That was different."

"Well never mind."

"I do mind. Suppose someone sees."

"There's nothing to see. Sue pulls the curtains."

"Sue? Ugh. What colour are her curtains?"

"Purple with silver and gold half and full moons. Lined of course."

"Of course. I wouldn't be surprised if she were a witch."

"What happened to Tommy Steele?"

"What indeed?"

The subject of Susan's life when she wasn't with me hung fire for several days. Mum was preoccupied with a crisis in Nurse Duggan's life. Their mongrel dog, Spike, had been hit by a car and needed his hip pinned. It had cost the Duggans a small fortune in vet's fees and mum couldn't understand why Nurse Duggan hadn't a) carried out the operation herself, or b) had the dog put down and bought a pedigree puppy with the money they would have saved.

"They could have had a Scottie dog. I wouldn't have minded her bringing it here as long as it was black. I can't abide white dogs."

"What about brown?"

"Scotties are never brown."

"But they all love Spike."

"Love. Put a puppy in a basket with a bow on its head and Spike could fly out of the window. Love's easily transferable you know."

Which eventually brought mum back to me, Susan, and Susan's secret life.

She suggested we follow Susan's Cortina in a mini-cab.

"I'll pay," she said. "If we lose her we could have our dinner out in the centre. There used to be a lovely fish and chip shop in Aycocks Green."

"That was over thirty years ago."

"It's probably a high-class seafood restaurant now. I know all about them. I follow the gourmet guide in the local paper. I could have battered kalamari and chips."

"They're called 'fries'."

She gave me her best withering look, "Joan, you impress me not a jot."

Susan has a lovely lounge. Well, the whole house is lovely. She has the money to get men in. But her lounge in particular; I think that's my favourite room as far as the decoration and furniture goes.

It's all peach, with the palest green and buttermilk. There's a white, fake fur rug in front of the mock, log-effect gas fire which should look tasteless but doesn't, and a three-piece suite she bought in Rackhams in Birmingham. Such soft leather, it's hard work getting up from.

Mum and I have a twenty-year-old red and black moquette settee and an intimate relationship with its springs. It was never modern, never anyone's first choice. It's the type of settee you throw something colourful over and cover with ethnic cushions, but mum says either, "When I die," ominously, or "It's an antique," in a smug manner that suggests that she knows something about antiques which I don't.

At the far end of Susan's lounge she's had mahogany-framed French windows put in – so expensive she had to get an extension on her considerable mortgage. When I asked her how much, egged on by mum, she clapped her hand to her forehead, rolled her eyes and said, "Never you mind, Joanie, leave the sleepless nights to me."

The French windows lead out on to a patio barbecue area. The barbecue is brick built, and surrounded by tubs of geraniums to make a feature of it when not in use. I'd never experienced it being used as Susan said it was too much of a fag for two, and the grill was a much better option under the circumstances. That summer she used it several times on Sunday afternoons running into evening. She said, "It's people from work. Very boring. You're well out of it."

I'd leant out of our top back bedroom window but it was impossible to see over two gardens and her slatted wood fence with its Nellie Moser Clematis which adds another three foot to the height. I gave up before mum spotted me from her seat in the garden, and went out and joined her with my book and a glass of cider.

Our garden is nice, but it's not as nice as Susan's. She has money and the car, while I have seed packets from Woolworths which go mouldy on the bathroom and kitchen windowsills because our house is damp. I could hear distant voices; Debbie Harry singing 'Sunday Girl', laughter, the chink of glasses. I could smell sausages. Mum was sitting in her deckchair contentedly shelling peas from a brown paper bag. Her little nose began to twitch in the balmy evening air.

"I thought she was a veggie," she said.

"It'll be for her guests."

"You think."

"Yes, I do think."

"You won't ask though."

"Relationships are built on trust."

"They're never built on someone being unable to say 'boo' to a goose."

"We talk about everything."

"Hah, she talks. You listen."

Those three barbecues that I wasn't invited to gently, almost imperceptibly, opened up a can of worms. Out they slithered as quiet as you like. Impossible to find and put back.

I told myself I was unreasonable and jealous. I read an article on self-esteem in mum's *Readers Digest* where a psychologist advised their readers to begin by valuing oneself – and if you behave like a doormat, you'll be taken for one. Then there was a letter on the problem page of her *Woman* magazine.

Q. *I think my husband is having an affair with another woman. He keeps going out in the evening and refuses to tell me where he's going, what he's doing, or who he's doing it with.*
A. *There may be a perfectly innocent reason for your husband's unexplained absences. Set aside a quiet time to discuss the matter. Tell him how hurt you are by his behaviour and explain that this is damaging the trust you have in him.*

I considered this carefully. Regretfully my problem didn't quite tally with this one. Susan hadn't refused to answer, she had been evasive. Now, if I put aside a 'quiet time to discuss the matter', it would mean she would know that I had suspicions. Nothing would ever be the same again between us. If Susan a) cared for me, but was slightly ashamed of my rustic lack of sophistication or b) – and for b) I had to take several deep breaths and brace myself – b) she was seeing another woman.

Well, I had no pride. I still didn't want to lose her and I would if I didn't maintain the fiction of trust between us. Almost worse would be c) me finding out her Tuesdays and Sundays were perfectly innocent, that she was playing Monopoly in a flat of muted colours while I would be exposed as a jealous possessive harpy, who had secretly har-boured resentment for a good part of a three-year relation-ship.

But if I followed her in a mini-cab? What could I achieve from a mini-cab? And once I started wondering that, the die was cast.

We planned the outing carefully. That's what it was to be if for any reason Susan spotted us. Mum convinced me that she was an absolute necessity on the journey.

"Where would you be off to on your own? Now with me, we could be going anywhere."

"At eight o'clock at night?" I asked.

"You're so provincial, Joan. The world and his wife go out at that time. There's jet-setters that don't go out for their dinner till midnight." She waved an inside page of *The News of the World* in my direction.

"Susan knows we're not jet-setters, nor are we the world and his wife."

"You've no imagination, Joan. Say it's a treat for me. We've been asked out by Nurse Duggan. She's got a maisonette off the Hagley Road."

At the time, put like that, it seemed quite reasonable.

Susan popped in every Sunday morning to deliver our newspapers. If she wasn't going out immediately, we had coffee and croissants together while mum lay in till twelve. That particular Sunday she seemed in no hurry to leave. I made one last attempt.

"Pity you're going out later, Sue, I'm feeling a bit depressed. Nearly the end of the summer. I haven't had a holiday in years. Me and mum will go on and on forever." Annoyingly, my eyes filled with tears.

"I'll bring in a takeaway tomorrow, Joan. Save us cooking. You can put your feet up. Perhaps we could get away for a few days in the autumn." She didn't sound enthusiastic, didn't even look up from her colour supplement. I tried again.

"Don't you miss seeing me, Tuesdays and Sundays?"

"I've got seeing you the next day to look forward to, lovey."

For the first time I resented the 'lovey'. I wasn't happy with the earlier 'Joan', either. It was a cold name. I'd always disliked it. Whenever Susan or mum used it instead of 'Joanie' they were either telling me off or mentally pushing me away. I'd never rowed with Susan, not once. I could feel bitter words burning on my tongue, desperate to spill out. I gulped down my coffee and stood up, began to gather the papers together. I didn't want her to know I was angry. I kept my voice light and friendly.

"I'm going to try and give mum a hairwash this afternoon. We're going out. Nurse Duggan's asked us around for a couple of hours."

At last Susan's head bobbed up from her magazine, "What's she like out of that uniform?"

"How should I know? She's very nice – kind and caring."

Susan turned a page, "She's married though. Kids too."

I tried a knowing smirk combined with a light laugh, "The married ones are the worst."

Immediately I felt hot with embarrassment. Poor Nurse Duggan. If she ever knew I'd said that about her. If Susan started making jokes, worse, innuendoes in front of mum. Susan hadn't noticed. She put the paper down and said in a surprisingly dispirited voice, "How will you get there? You'll never get the old lady on a bus?"

"Good heavens. As if. We've a mini-cab collecting us. No problem."

She looked unconvinced. Followed me across the kitchen to the sink, pushing her hands in and out of the pockets of her stone-coloured jeans.

"Joanie, I'm sorry. If I'd known, I'd have driven you. Why not put it off till next Saturday?"

For that I gave her a good, hard kiss. I felt better. She looked genuinely anxious. She cared – it was as simple as that.

"We'll be fine in a cab. Now off you go, I've got to have my bath."

"Can I stay and scrub your back?"

"What if I said yes?"

"Saucy," she said and hugged me.

I watched her walk jauntily down our path. At the gate she gave me her usual careless wave and off she went without looking back. Mum was right, she did swagger, she did look mighty pleased with herself. She took it for granted that women were all like me. It was easy to be mad about her; that's what turned my heart over.

I almost didn't go. It was mum. She was so excited about the outing. It hadn't occurred to me that she was unhappy, until I saw her happy. I felt guilty that I never took her out. I could organise trips. I could do more.

She let me wash her hair, which didn't make the water as dirty as I'd expected. I felt very fond of her skinny grey neck and bony shoulders. I gave her a blowdry and she didn't complain as she usually did that I'd made her look like a mad woman when it refused to return to its usual moulded curls and waves. I made her up with lotions and founda-tions, powder and blusher, highlighted her brow bone and didn't have to force her to put in her teeth. She wore a blue wool dress that I'd bought for her several Christmases ago. I drew the line at a hat.

"No one wears hats these days. We don't want to draw attention to ourselves."

Her face fell.

"Anyway you look lovely, mum, look in the mirror."

"I look like an old has-been."

"Well that's better than a never-has-been. Now what am I going to wear?"

"Go in disguise," she said, too charmed by her own reflection to be interested in my clothes.

I'd imagined Susan spotting us straight away, especially with the metal sign proclaiming 'DON'S MINI-CAB SER-VICES' plus telephone number in red attached to Don's roof rack. I'd imagined Don losing her at the first roundabout and me having to search out mum's fish restaurant in Aycocks Green. I'd even imagined Don evincing curiosity and immediately asking awkward questions. That came later. Susan didn't even glance in our direction as she sped past, heading towards the High Street. I said, "Follow that car please," and Don shot off in hot pursuit as if all his days were spent thus.

I sat in the back. Don and mum in the front were nattily synchronised. He looked more like a possible son to this elegant old lady than I a daughter. He wore good grey trousers, a tweed jacket, white shirt and a rather nice tie with an emblem. His hair was short and greying, cut straight across at the back, exposing an inch of tidy tanned neck.

I'd reverted to one of my early navy jogging suits and trainers. I'd fought the temptation to bring my black rubber torch and lost. It gave me confidence, nestling against my thigh on the seat next to me.

We drove out of Birmingham in quite affable silence. I began to think the ride was almost pleasant... we might pass Susan being welcomed at the entrance of a block of flats by a loving couple with a Monopoly board somewhere in evidence and my suspicions would be laid to rest. I'd say, "There you are mum," and "What did I tell you?" and then, what the hell, we'd have dinner in a country pub. Even ask Don to join us for a drink perhaps. He seemed to pick up that he was in my thoughts; I caught his eye in the driving mirror.

"Your friend's very boyish," he said.

"Masculine," mum said, "She looks like Tommy Steele."

I gave him a weak smile. Mum wasn't leaving it there. She was having no misunderstanding about Susan or our motives.

"She's no friend of my daughter's. The little devil's got her talons into my son-in-law," she said.

"Ah," said Don, making a smooth right.

"He swings both ways."

"Does he?" Don again.

"Don't be ridiculous, mum." I tapped her shoulder warningly.

"Not ridiculous at all. The last one was hardly out of short trousers."

"Disgusting."

"Mother, will you keep quiet. She exaggerates. I know nothing for certain. She's his business colleague. Probably perfectly innocent. My husband and I are very happily married."

I stared at my ringless hand and then back up to Don in the driving mirror; his eyes were warm with angry sympathy.

"My wife," he paused to round a roundabout and came dangerously close to the back of Susan's car, "Went off with another woman. You just don't know what goes on in this world."

Even mum quietened down after that. He'd rather stolen her thunder. She stared out of the window, her washed white curls moving gently from side to side. I thought apprehensively, "She'll have a fine story for Nurse D tomorrow," and thanked god that Nurse D knew better than to believe a word mum said, although she was excellent at simulation. She had a natural ability to use words and phrases in response to mum, so completely outside her normal vocabulary that they made her performance credible.

"Good grief" and "What a sod, deserves a good pasting", "I'm in your corner, Mrs Littler." Only once had she overplayed her hand, when she'd asked to be "buggered with a left-handed broom", and mum and I had looked so shocked, she'd gone scarlet and added quickly, "In a manner of speaking."

"She's going off the motorway, I think she's heading towards Coventry," Don said, cutting across my reverie, and we pulled out of the main line of traffic and followed, keeping one or two cars between us both.

It was nearly eight o'clock and beginning to get dark. The road narrowed into a single lane on each side. Don switched on his headlamps as we drove along between high hedges. The cars ahead of us turned off; Susan was about a hundred yards in front, the silver-grey paintwork of her Cortina glimmering indistinctly in the failing light. She slowed at a junction, signalled and turned left.

By the time we reached the junction, the road was empty. We drove on to the next fork in the road; still no sign of her. Don pulled into a layby and we resumed eye contact.

"Perhaps we should go home," I said hopefully.

"What about supper?" mum asked.

"If we see somewhere nice, we could stop."

"What about my fish and chip restaurant?" she persisted.

"By the time we get all the way back to Aycocks Green,

it'll be too late to eat, mum," I said. "What do you think, Don?"

"Bit of an anticlimax," he answered moodily. He turned the car around and we drove back down the road in silence. He drove slowly. I could tell that neither he nor mum wanted to give up. He looked to the right, she to the left.

Mum thumped the dashboard, "There it is. That's where she's gone," and Don skidded to an emergency stop in the half-concealed opening of a drive. Invisible from the road was a sign, 'Penlea House. Hotel and Licensed Restaurant.'

"There's no point going in there, she'll see us," I said.

"But Joanie, we must. We've come all this way. I'm hungry."

"We could give her a few minutes, then follow," said Don.

"No Don. I can hardly go into a hotel dressed like this."

A Jaguar rolled up behind us and hooted politely. We had no choice. Don drove in. The car park was almost full. There was no sign of Susan. Her deserted Cortina was tucked snugly in between a Mercedes and a Volvo estate. Don parked the Corsair in the shadow of the fir-tree hedge and switched on the light over the mirror.

"Well," he said, slapping the wheel with both hands, "What now?"

"I need to use the Ladies," said mum primly.

"But mum, I can't take you in there. Look at me."

"Don's very smart. She'll never recognise me done up to the nines and with a young man."

Don smirked at me in the mirror, "Might as well."

"You won't let my mother speak to anyone or make trouble? Just in and out."

"I've not brought my tablets, Joan. I must have a snack or there'll be all hell let loose."

"Don't worry, Mrs Er... I'll get your mother a bowl of soup or similar."

"They won't let you have just a bowl of soup in a posh place like that," I remonstrated.

"Or similar, Joan. Don said 'or similar'."

I gave up. "It's really very good of you, Don," I simpered.

He smiled proudly, "All part of the job," and "We aim to please. Are you fit, Mrs Littler?"

"Fit as I'll ever be."

She shook her head girlishly and patted her curls at the back. I said disapprovingly, "You'll need some cash, mum."

"Oh, I've got money," she shook her leather handbag in my direction.

"Not enough for this place. It's not a shilling's worth of fish and a threepenny bag of chips." I handed two ten-pound notes to Don.

"They'll think Don's your toy boy if you pay."

Mum tittered and Don looked momentarily embarrassed, but not for long. He jumped out of the car, and opened mum's door with a flourish. She was obviously making an effort and swung her thin legs out quite gracefully, then let him heave her upright. They began to walk away, arm in arm; I was quite forgotten. I leant out of my window, and shouted, "Good luck. Be careful," in a cheerful manner. They half turned and waved, then off they went again – Don steering mum between the cars towards a flight of grand stone steps that led up to open baronial doors. He looked tall and youthful next to mum. She'd have liked a son. I could imagine a son being much more entertaining than I was. Not as much use, but somehow being useful never receives a high score on the 'What makes you like someone?' questionnaire.

Mum was leaning heavily on his arm, shuffling. I couldn't be absolutely certain but 'shuffling' implied she still had her carpet slippers on. Her feet were the one area I hadn't checked. They weren't just any old slippers, they were a begrudged birthday present from Susan. Black velvet with pink embroidered roses. I'd forced her to order them from Burlington's catalogue.

I wound up my window. I felt very tired, hungry and a little chilly. On Don's back car shelf I found a tartan travel rug and I wound it around my shoulders. From my bag I took out the small notebook and biro I'd brought along with the intention of taking notes. At that moment I couldn't envisage the state of mind I'd been in to think I'd need such items.

No more cars arrived. The car park was quiet except for the distant strains of 'Tea for Two Cha-Cha' which ran into 'Ferry 'Cross the Mersey', in slow foxtrot time. I tried to name every tune, their original singer and possible composers. Then I jotted down interesting car numbers, how many cars to a visible row. I drew out a small plan of the front of the building in relation to the road, and began work on an imagined version of the back. I drew in a rose garden with arbour, fountain, swimming pool and finally a helipad.

After an hour or so, I fell asleep and dreamt that I was hurrying along a busy road, wearing one of mum's old nightdresses. I was hot with embarrassment over a large darn on the bodice. I kept repeating, "What will Susan say?" over and over as I approached an angry crowd, who were trying to turn over a grey Corsair.

At that point I woke up. The crowd turned into two wide men in dark suits and bow ties, with faces so squashed and broken they had to be bouncers. They reminded me of the men on the door of the Bingo Hall that mum and I had gone to when I was between thirteen and fifteen, whom she'd insisted were really very nice men when you got talking to them. This pair didn't seem particularly keen on talking. One of them appeared to be bouncing mum up and down on the bonnet of the car, but ten seconds later, when I'd grown more alert, I realised he was actually trying to restrain her from bouncing up and down on the bonnet.

The other chap held on to Don, who looked as light and flimsy as a rag doll. His nice tie had disappeared and his shirt was flapping out of his trousers. He was shouting in a very impressive manner, "Take your filthy hands off Mrs Littler. My client could have a heart attack at any moment."

I almost clapped. I almost shouted, "Bravo, admirable, courageous." Mum was ahead of me. Her voice, high and excited, rose above Don and the sound of scuffling.

"I have angina. I'll speak to my MP."

The man let her go and she slithered sideways.

"If your heart's bad, you shouldn't be drinking, lady," he said menacingly, heading around to my side of the car. He jerked open the door.

"Your mother and her pal," he stated sneeringly, with a difficult backward nod towards them. "Would you take over, please?" He emphasised the 'please', unpleasantly.

I was almost as tall as he was, nowhere near the width, but my height gave me confidence. I walked around to the front of the car and inspected mum as if I was picking her out of a police line-up.

"Yes. This is my mother. Mum, are you all right?"

"Oh, I've had a lovely time," she said.

"You're lucky we didn't call the police." Her bouncer moved restlessly on the balls of his feet. I sensed he was just looking for an excuse to punch someone hard. Don felt the same way. His bravado had disappeared and he looked as if he might cry. Mum was still chipper, propped in place on the bonnet. She surveyed her male trio with a coquettish tipsy smile and began to swing one leg to a height of about eighteen inches from the ground. On the third swing, she sent her slipper spinning away across the gravel. Don raised his eyes heavenwards and got back in the car.

"We want you lot out of here now – and go quietly." A pudgy forefinger jabbed at my breastbone. I wasn't listening. Someone had picked up mum's slipper and was putting it carefully back on her foot. I didn't recognise the dark suit, the ruffled shirt or the scarlet cummerbund, but the glossy hair, long enough to tuck behind her neat ears. I knew that hair; how it felt. Soft as silk between my fingers, cool against my hot cheek. I mumbled "Susan," and hated myself for sniffing. She looked up at me with a half-smile, her eyes regretful.

"I'll speak to you tomorrow evening, Joan."

She turned and walked away.

"Pooh to Sue," mum shouted after her.

"Get in the car, mum, now."

Half pushing, half lifting, I manhandled her into her seat and threw her handbag on to the floor at her feet. Don made no effort to help. He stared straight ahead, one hand on the ignition, the other gripping the steering wheel. In the orange light, I could see his forehead was shiny with sweat. He started the engine and I had to nip quickly into my seat at the back. He would have left me behind, I could read it in his expression.

The two bouncers watched us go. We moved past Susan, past a woman in a satin evening dress, its colour exactly matching Susan's cummerbund. The woman shaded her eyes from our headlights with her hand. The beam caught the gleam of several rings and a heavy bracelet.

My face was pressed to the window. I wanted to see my rival. She wasn't pretty. She was beautiful. She looked rich and cared for. I couldn't blame Susan, there was no contest.

After about five minutes of silent driving, Don produced a handkerchief and mopped his face. We resumed eye contact.

"That was very upsetting for me," he said bitterly, "It brought back unpleasant memories."

Mum said nothing. From her guttural congested breathing, I assumed she was either asleep or dying. At that moment, I didn't care which. I didn't much care about Don's upset, but felt obliged to say, "Sorry about that, Don."

"Well, you say 'sorry', but I wonder how sorry you really are?"

A flicker of surprise penetrated my blanket of misery at the amount of mental rapport Don and I seemed to share. Another time and place and we might have enjoyed a cordial discussion on telepathy in a homely pub over pints of local beer.

"What exactly happened?" I asked weakly, hoping talk might purge away some of his resentment.

It's strange that however unhappy one is, the practicalities of life still intrude. The prospect of Don's bill at the end of the evening had the power to pierce my unhappiness. How to mollify him? Mum was the man mollifier, but she was slumped against the window, except when we went around corners, then she fell sideways and slumped against Don.

"Because your mother was ill," said Don, in a sarcastic, brittle voice, "or so she said, they gave us a plate of sandwiches and a pot of tea. They couldn't have been nicer. Settled us in a quiet spot behind some potted palms because obviously we were unsuitably dressed for a ball.

"Your mother said her heart needed stimulation, she pulled awful faces and said she was about to have a funny turn, so I had to go to the bar on the next floor up to buy two double Jamesons. No water for Mrs Littler, thank you."

"Look Don, I really am sorry. If it's all too painful…"

"We then had two more double Jamesons."

"Why?"

Don fell silent. I understood. There isn't necessarily a sensible reason for some actions. When he was sure that I appreciated this fact, he continued, his voice growing quieter and colder.

"I returned from a visit to the Gentlemen's toilet and found your mother haranguing a couple at a central table. Of course I didn't recognise her – your friend. She'd changed her clothes. From the back I thought she was a man. Your mother was so incensed, I assumed this person to be your husband with yet another woman. However, when I realised the true situation, it set something off inside me. As I said, it brought up unpleasant memories. I behaved in an unprofessional manner. I let myself down. Lost my temper. Without going into due detail – do you understand?"

"I think so."

"I don't like lesbians. I have my reasons. No one's fault. Well, someone's fault. Not necessarily yours. However, on consideration, I don't like you. I thought I did, but I don't."

When we reached the house, Don helped me get mum out of his car, and we supported her between us as far as the front door – she seemed to have lost the use of her legs.

"Will you be all right with her?" he asked stiffly.

"Yes, thank you. How much do I owe you?"

"Nothing. I don't want your money."

"But that's ridiculous. Look here..." But he was already halfway down our path.

I sat for the last time in Susan's lounge, alone on the four-seater settee, hugging a mug of coffee. She paced the fake fur rug – cigarette in one hand, a small cut glass ashtray in the other.

"Did I ever make any promises, Joan?"

"No."

"Or tell you that I loved you?"

I thought about that one for a minute.

"You were very affectionate."

"There's a world of difference between love and affection."

"I'm not a fool, Susan, nor am I completely in the wrong. The fact is you've lied to me – consistently." I added 'consistently' to back up the lying accusation, in case that alone sounded insubstantial.

"I told you what you wanted to hear," she said.

"How very convenient," I muttered, almost to myself.

"And to send your mother and that homophobic buffoon in to do your dirty work..."

"I wasn't dressed for it," I said feebly.

"Your mother was in her carpet slippers."

"Would you have preferred her to be wearing a fur stole and patent stilettos?"

Susan dabbed out her cigarette, her lips began to twitch. It was funny, the image of mum in her slippers and bouncy

curls, Don with his tweed jacket and self-pity. We both started laughing. I said, "Susan, I'm sorry I didn't send them in
better dressed, but you know the state of our finances."

She spluttered, "If it had even been Nurse Duggan. At
least a uniform."

She put the ashtray on the mantelpiece and sat down facing me, the width of a seat between us. Gently she took my
hand in hers.

"Oh Joanie, I'm sorry. It was my fault. I knew it couldn't
last forever, but we've had a good run, haven't we?"

"So, I'm the one that gets the elbow?"

"I couldn't lose Caroline."

"Why don't you live with her?"

"She's married. She's not happy but she won't leave him,
there's a child involved. One day I'll be the one who gets
dumped when things get too hot for her."

"Won't you miss me?"

She let go of my hand and stood up; very businesslike,
her expression hardening.

"We could be friends," I said.

"No, it's over. I can't risk it."

I put down the mug on the glass table top, for once not
on the china coaster. At the front door I shouted, "I'll see
myself out then?"

I heard her moving in the lounge. I knew the sounds;
flipping a cigarette from the packet, flicking a flame from
her lighter – inhaling.

"Look after yourself, lovey," she called.

TWO
1981
Just mother and me

There was nothing and no one left for me in Birmingham. I couldn't believe it at first – that Susan could switch from padded Valentines, eighteen inches high with "Be mine forever", to not even stopping her car for me to cross on a zebra. If she hadn't recognised me with the added weight, she must have known it was my shopping trolley. I'd spent several afternoons the previous year, while mum was asleep, customising the Black Watch tartan canvas with silver lurex stars. Spot it and I was never far behind, but no, suddenly, the trolley and I had both become invisible.

The 'SOLD' board was up in her front garden, but her car was still parked in the drive every day. I dreaded the removal lorry arriving while I was in, dreaded the removal lorry arriving while I was out – coming back to find her house empty, the lined purple curtains on their way to destinations unknown. Then I fell out with Mrs Botolph.

***

Mrs Botolph had moved in next door a couple of years after I was born. I don't remember her arrival – it seemed she had been there for ever. Hers was the attached house rather than the house on the other side of the alleyway. We'd had a chap called Howard living *there* for about ten years. He said he was a zoologist, backing this up by wearing khaki safari suits, winter and summer.

When I was a child and had no say in the matter we'd stuck to mum's 'I like a wild garden' policy. This was a vicarious view as she rarely ventured out into the garden, but gave the weeds her tacit approval from the open kitchen window as she smilingly tipped grouts from the teapot down the outside wall. (Teabags were a long time arriving at our house.) Sometimes when it was really warm, mum sat in the back doorway, her skirt tucked into her knickers, dropping ash from her cigarette into our partially blocked drain and saying something like "Nature really feeds the soul, Joan," as if she was telling me a known medical fact.

I put a stop to nature having so much of its own way when I moved home again from London. Susan – once Susan and I romantically took wings and flew – became my horticultural adviser.

"No rules, Joanie love, and what do we have? Chaos. Same with gardening. I understand a wild garden – in touch with nature. Like the theory; two out of ten for practicality. Wild flowers are weeds, end of story. If I were in your shoes, I'd go for flowering shrubs and foliage plants. Keep it simple, sweetheart."

That's how she talked to me in those halycon days;

sweethearts and lovies littered her conversation. Ho-hum.

We hired a man to prune the two plane trees – they stood like two muscle-bound weightlifters on guard at the bottom of the garden. Together we cleared the weeds and the wildness, fences became fences again, we turfed the lawn and dug beds to a depth of two spades. Plants grew where I put them and remained the size and shape that I wanted. Only the buddleia remained.

"Get rid, Joan. No room for sentimentality in a garden this size" – which summed up Susan's eventual attitude to me. But I held on to the buddleia because it was magical, a wonder in an otherwise often dreary life with its clouds of red admirals, commas and cabbage-white butterflies fluttering and settling on pale mauve spires. Each spring I chopped it back and every summer it spread its heavy leafed branches cheerfully out over our garden, over Mrs Botolph's garden.

Let me make this clear, my rift with Mrs B had been on the cards for years. We neither of us liked the cut of the other's jib, but because of mum, a glowering peace was maintained. It was a baking hot Thursday in late August. I was lying under our buddleia, worrying out a deep-rooted dandelion, minding my own business, and thinking what a rare pleasure it was to find a weed to deal with in our tidy garden.

Had she bothered to look over the fence that afternoon, she might not have seen me, but she would have certainly seen the soles of my trainers and my yellow and black striped socks. That she didn't bother to look was typical of her 'I am

Birmingham's first lady' attitude, which had irked me since being told to pick up my sweet wrappers as a schoolgirl.

Suddenly the fence began to shake, and I could hear and feel her vigorously clipping away above my head.

"This damn and blasted bush," she said angrily, as if the bush had been playing her up all afternoon and by golly was going to be taught a lesson. "I'll have a word with Dolly. My whole garden is overshadowed. The caterpillars are having a field day on my sweetpeas."

"Why don't you speak to Joan?"

I recognised the musical notes of Mrs B's rather attractive young granddaughter, Gemma. Her voice floated towards me from somewhere near their house.

"Joan, pah, I don't speak to Joan," clip, clip, "any more than I can help. She makes Dolly's life a misery."

"Surely not. She seems quite nice, in an old-fashioned way."

My admiration for Gemma, a fire previously fed by the hope that she secretly admired me, fizzled and went out.

"How old is she anyway, Gran?"

"About forty-five."

"She can't be."

"Well forty then, she looks forty-five."

"Gran, leave that bush for now, you're getting covered in butterflies – it's like a horror film. Come and have a drink."

I peered through a knothole and saw Mrs B's secateurs bounce on to her shadowed lawn, her well-padded hips in yellow crimplene slacks retreat towards her French windows. I stared at the secateurs; surely they were mine? A present from Susan when she'd bought me the rose bush. How typical. Mrs B was always on the borrow. Each Friday morning she insinuated herself into our kitchen for a coffee. Never left empty-handed.

Once mum had lent her my stainless steel spade. After several requests from me for its return, she'd left it in our porch caked in mess from Rusty, her recently purchased Highland terrier. She never took him for a walk, just let him out in the garden and went around once a month with a shovel – or on that occasion, having probably lost her own shovel, my new spade.

Mum had said, "People with breeding don't get uptight about dog's mess."

I'd said, "People with breeding have no respect for other people or their property."

I could see Mrs Botolph's painted toenails from my spyhole in the fence. She was in a reclining position on a lounger, waving her plump tanned feet at the sun; two flimsy gold sandals were perched on an upturned flowerpot.

"Actually the daughter's gay," she said.

"Joan, the name's Joan," I mouthed against the fence.

"She's not, is she?"

"She is. An absolute monster. Dolly's told me dreadful stories. Doll, in bed, half dead with dehydration, calling out for a glass of milk, water, anything. All she gets is 'In a minute', from Joan at the foot of the stairs. Half an hour before the glass of water appears, with Dolly almost unconscious by then. Daughter been canoodling on the telephone with a female stock controller from Homebase."

There was a pause in the conversation and the gurgling sound of straws being dragged across the bottom of their glasses.

"More Pimm's, Gemma?"

"Just a teensy. She can't hear us, can she?"

"No. The television's on next door. I can hear it. She's watching tennis. Chris Evert's playing Martina Navratilova. She's another one."

"Chris Evert?"

"No, the one with the horse face. They're always unattractive."

"Oh, I know, but you can overlook it when they're good at something."

To think I'd actually imagined I liked Gemma. I rose with difficulty through the branches and propped my chin on the top of the fence. "Excuse me, Mrs Botolph, when you can spare a minute, are those my secateurs?"

Gemma blushed prettily and sank her red face into her empty glass. Mrs Botolph, because of her breeding, was a tougher nut. She took a jaunty suck at her straw before replying, "If they belong to anyone, they belong to your sainted mother."

"Well on her behalf, could I have them back please?"

She shuffled into her sandals and ambled slowly towards me, stopping to dead-head a dahlia en route. As I took the secateurs from her I hissed, "You're a bigot, Mrs Botolph."

She yawned in my face and drawled, "This bush wants cutting down. It's an eyesore."

In our small living room, mum had pulled the curtains

against the sun; her chair was drawn up to the television set.

"Have you been complaining about me to Mrs Botolph?" I asked.

"Possibly."

I slumped into the adjacent armchair and put my feet on the coffee table. Mum twitched with disapproval.

"Who's winning then, mum?"

"Martina of course. Get me a shandy."

After the match, we moved back into the kitchen. Mum sat at the table idling over a general knowledge crossword puzzle while I washed lettuce and tomatoes for our tea. Crosswords had become her main hobby over the last year; I'd bought her an ancient set of encyclopedias, a large-print Bible and several second-hand dictionaries. There was talk of cancelling her *Reader's Digest* subscription and ordering *National Geographic* instead.

On Mrs B's rabble-rousing Friday morning visits, she always brought in her puzzle magazines which she'd already done, writing the answers in with pencil, then rubbing them out again. Sometimes the longer words were still visible.

"Obligingly," mum said.

"Patronisingly," was my interpretation.

I said she wanted mum to see she'd known the answers, or she assumed mum needed help and wouldn't know the answers as she'd lived all her life in the Birmingham area with no husband to speak of.

Mrs Botolph's late husband, of whom we'd seen many photographs and heard much, had been a Wing Commander. Mum always nodded admiringly at all the anecdotes, even on the third or fourth rendering, but was still not quite certain what being a Wing Commander meant.

"Well, it's obviously Air Force," she said.

"Obviously, mum."

"I think Laurence Olivier was one in a war film in the forties. He certainly wore a flying jacket with a fur collar."

"That's a big help, then."

We had many conversations like that.

"Joan, how do you spell 'comedienne'?" she asked.

"I don't know, but can I have your attention, please?"

"Not at the moment. Busy, busy, busy."

"Mrs Botolph says I make your life a misery."

"You can be tricky."

"That's not quite the same. You told her about Jennifer from Homebase."

"Well, it was news. I don't go out anywhere. I have to keep my end up conversation-wise."

She began flipping through her Bible, reading the headings of each page through her black-handled magnifying glass.

"Did you tell her about P Rogers as well?"

"There's something about donkeys in Jeremiah, and yes I did tell her about P Rogers. Really Joan, when I can't even go into my own bank because you're having a one-sided flirtation with one of the counter staff and don't want people to know you look after your mother. Here we are," she said triumphantly, "Wild asses stand on the bare heights and sniff the wind as wolves do."

"What?"

"Wild asses. Ten down; four and five letters."

She closed the Bible and laid down her magnifying glass.

"I wish you'd get me into Shepherd's Fennel. I could keep Mrs Scott company and you could have your own life." She sighed and her head drooped forward over her magazine.

"But you'd hate being in a residential home. There's no freedom."

"There's no freedom here."

The conversation was taking an unwelcome downward turn; usually mum and I kept our serious thoughts to ourselves.

"And Mrs Scott's going senile – you said so yourself. She kept calling you 'Old Scottie' last time we visited her."

"That's because she doesn't see me every day like she used to. She's my oldest friend, Joan. And Mrs Botolph. She'd visit each week. She's promised."

"More like a threat. I wouldn't want her visiting me."

Mum sighed and went back to her crossword puzzle.

"Tuna fish or boiled potatoes?" I asked her.

"I'm not bothered."

"What if we got a cat?"

"I don't like cats. If it comes near me, it'll feel the toe of my slipper."

She looked up at me and grinned; a really young grin that lit up her face.

"You could have been a comedienne, mum. You still make me laugh."

"Yes. I've thought that myself from time to time. I'd have

liked to tread the boards. A talent wasted." She picked up her biro and began to study 'Clues Down'. "Mind you, that Susan seemed to find you amusing. I could hear her from down the garden, roaring away at something you said. She was a funny bugger. You're better off."

She picked up a dictionary from the stack of books leaning against the table leg. It was very quiet in the kitchen; I tossed slices of tomatoes into the salad bowl. We both suppressed sighs.

THREE

1982/83

The fallow years

Early May; blue sky, sun struggling through good-natured clouds – summer definitely in the air – me at the kitchen sink contemplating my doom. It was Friday morning. On Friday mornings I went to Sainsbury's. They knew me in Sainsbury's. If I missed a week, Elspeth, my preferred till lady, said, "We missed you last week, Joan. Mum poorly?" All the queue would give me sympathetic looks and let me take as long as I liked to pack my carrier bags. Life stretched out in front of me; Elspeth would retire, would be replaced, the replacement would get married and her children would have Saturday jobs there, and I'd get older and older and no one would remember that I'd ever been young.

"Mrs Botolph will be in, in a minute," mum said, intent on cutting articles and quiz pages from the local paper.

"I'm not stopping her," I said, intent on my barren future and chipping limescale from the base of our mixer taps.

"You'll put her off. She'll be ill at ease. She never got over you calling her 'a bigot'."

"She is a bigot. Anyway, Mrs Botolph's never ill at ease. I

could sit stark naked on the draining board and she wouldn't bat an eyelid."

"She'd have something to say about it when you'd left the room, though."

"I can imagine."

I exchanged the bread knife for a rusty skewer.

"You'll be late for Sainsbury's."

"Mother," I said as the point of the skewer slipped and gouged a two-inch scratch into the non–stainless steel sink, "There's no way I can be late for Sainsbury's. They don't close till eight p.m. It is now ten-thirty a.m. Anyway, I don't have to go to Sainsbury's today."

"What about my broccoli and spinach? Nurse Duggan says I must have my green veg."

"There's enough green veg in the fridge to take us to August Bank Holiday and there's spring greens almost ready in the garden."

"I don't like what you grow. It tastes bitter."

"Bitter is good for you. Bitter means there's plenty of vitamins and iron present. I'll get any necessities from the corner shop."

"I see." She clicked her false teeth annoyingly.

"What do you see?"

"I see an excuse to march past her ladyship's house."

"If you're talking about Susan, she moved out months ago."

That quietened her for at least a minute. I suppressed a smile. I knew what she was thinking: "Poor old Joan... what she's gone through... only, Mrs B due in any minute now, rabid for a cup of coffee... no time to sit Joan down and offer sympathy and a paper tissue."

"It's all right, mum. Susan is a faint and distant memory." I shrugged my left shoulder several times to ease the slight discomfort I felt somewhere in the breastbone area. "No, I'm not bothered any more. Only, I've been thinking about you and me – in the future, things may have to change."

"Things?" She wrinkled up her nose as if I'd put a plate of raw liver in front of her. "I don't think I've time to talk about 'things' this morning."

"Well, lucky old you."

Skewer chucked in sink. Bugger the limescale. Most women my age wouldn't even know of the existence of limescale. Were mornings like this to be the apogees of my life?

'Apogee', another word I shouldn't necessarily know. No, I wasn't ready for cosy afternoons with mum, poring over dictionaries and encyclopedias, gleaning some small excitement from how to spell 'dirigible', and knowing the sixteenth US president, emancipator of slaves and assassination victim. Seven and seven.

I left mum sharpening pencils and went out into the garden. The perennial geraniums needed dividing, better late than never. There was potting up and cutting back to do; jobs I'd neglected for almost a year. I'd been too despondent to do any more than keep the lawn mown and the beds weeded. I got my wellington boots from the shed, lined up fork, spade, trowel and dibber, felt chilly and set off back to the kitchen for my jacket.

The door was bolted. I went round to the window. Mrs Botolph was already ensconced, spreading unfamiliar butter, half an inch thick, on to unfamiliar scones. I tapped on the glass: "Mum can't eat that. She's on a strict diet."

They both looked up. Mrs B waved half a scone in my direction before popping it into her mouth. Mum said, "Yum, yum. Buzz off, Joan."

"Can I come in? I need my coat," I shouted.

Mrs Botolph lumbered over to the window and opened it a couple of inches.

"We'll pass it out to you."

"But I want to come in."

"You can't." Mum from the table. "We're discussing things, Joan."

"You said you didn't have time to discuss 'things'." Mrs Botolph passed over my jacket. "And mum shouldn't be eating butter or refined flour," I said.

"Gardening, Joan." She closed the window and went back to the table. From her red patent handbag she took a cardboard file and began spreading pages of estate agents' details out in front of mum. I recognised them, recognised the file. This was one of Mrs Botolph's hobbies: going around strangers' houses and pretending she loved their decor and intended to make an offer the minute she got back home.

Years ago, when I was quite small, and mum still able to stride up hill and down dale, we'd spent many Saturdays disrupting lunches and afternoon teas, wandering from room to room, tapping walls and enquiring about party fences as if our possible purchase depended on it.

Mrs Botolph saying, "Now this is nice, Dolly."

Mum saying, "Very nice, Mrs Botolph."

Me saying nothing.

"Nothing changes," I thought sagely. I returned to my spread of tools. The sun shone on the gleaming tines of my fork, the polished surface of the trowel – they were far too clean to get dirty today.

"I will go to the corner shop for necessities and cake," I thought.

Of course, mum was right. I couldn't help myself. I stopped outside Susan's house. The lined purple curtains with their moons and stars were long gone, now there were crisp white nets at the windows. The front door was painted a sombre navy, no longer a rich polished mahogany, and all that remained of the welcoming brass carriage lamp, which mum said was the sign of an intrinsically common person, were a couple of dangling wires. Everything was different. Another personality imposed on the house.

It hadn't taken the garden so very long to return to the wild. Susan had always had a fight on her hands with the bindweed, and now it twisted tightly around the branches of her laurel hedge, pale green tendrils waving loosely in the breeze. Her once manicured lawn was studded with dandelion rosettes and clumps of couch grass. The roses looked sickly and hadn't been pruned. I tutted over foreseen future ravages: mildew, black spot, who would control the aphids now?

I plunged my arm into the laurel almost up to my armpit and began to pull at the convolvulus: tight, sinuous stems winding around the rough bark. Suddenly the front door opened and out came a man in a suit – would-be executive type, possible assistant manager of a supermarket. Sainsbury's? No, I'd have recognised him.

"Er, yes?" he said, pausing at his gate.

"Sorry. I harbour a grudge against bindweed. It's a menace."

"Really?"

I retrieved my arm and stood awkwardly with my fist full of weed and laurel twigs.

As a rule, men don't look at me. They look at my jacket, my shoes (in this case, wellingtons). I think by then they assume the face isn't worth bothering about.

"You're not by any chance a gardener," he said, eyes fixed on the dried mud caking the toes of my boots.

"Actually, I am." I moved one boot in a small graceful arc, ballerina fashion, to discompose any rugged perceptions he might have assumed. "I lodge with Mrs Littler, two doors down. She's one of my regular customers. You won't have seen her, she's an invalid."

"What do you charge?"

"Two pounds fifty an hour."

"That much?"

"Two pounds for cash."

His face cleared. He rested his briefcase on the bonnet of a dusty Vauxhall Estate and considered the distant townscape.

"You don't wash cars as well, do you?"

My chin rose proudly. "No, I do not. I'm Wisley trained. A member of the Royal Horticultural Society. In London you'd pay a small fortune for my services."

He looked impressed. Dusted off his briefcase and came to a decision.

"You couldn't make a start today? Just knock the front into shape, perhaps start on the back. My girlfriend and her family are staying for the weekend. First impressions. You know."

I stroked my chin thoughtfully, looked at the sky, looked at my watch and bid goodbye to the Eccles cakes in the corner shop.

"Do you have your own equipment?" I felt both our faces redden.

"The previous owner left everything: lawnmower, hose, spade, forks, the lot. Didn't take a thing as far as I can see. Immaculate. Didn't need it where she was going."

"Where was she going?" I asked, loosening, then tightening my watch strap nonchalantly.

"America. Did you know her?"

"Slightly."

"Seemed a pleasant woman. Quite masculine looking, but pleasant."

"Mmm," I said.

TAPE 2

Joan: That was my very first paid gardening job.

Q: You didn't feel uncomfortable with a lie?

Joan: Not at all. I've always felt comfortable with lies – telling the truth's been my downfall. One makes oneself vulnerable, if I can be serious for a moment.

Q: You're not often serious, are you, Joan?

Joan: People switch off.

Q: People?

Joan: Friends, lovers, mum. Edith can be quite sympathetic.

Q: In what way?

Joan: She has a sympathetic stare. Something of the 'I can only guess at what you've had to suffer, Joan' stare.

Q: You're joking again. Have you always made 'people' laugh?

Joan: It's an approval thing. Not like mum, who had a natural witty sarcasm. She wasn't bothered who liked her or didn't, just said what she felt. At school I was useless – all I could do was make jokes, even the teachers laughed.

Q: When did you decide you wanted to use your talent career-wise?

Joan: I'm not a 'career-wise' person. Everything evolves or it doesn't. I had daydreams: I'd be on the 73 bus, exchanging quips with the conductor and some comedy moghul's assistant would *be sitting across the aisle. "Here's my card. You're brilliant. We're auditioning for new talent, Thursday."*

Q: *That never happened?*

Joan: *No. Bus conductors don't like me.*

Q: *I'm tempted to ask why, perhaps later. Tell me, when did you start writing, seriously?*

Joan: *After the Sandy Banks interlude.*

Q: *Person? Place?*

Joan: *I'll tell you the story.*

Q: *Another mother story?*

Joan: *Yes and no.*

FOUR
1985
Lest I forget Sandy Banks

If I'd understood mum correctly, a 'fanny merchant' was someone who looked impressive, inspired confidence, yet failed to come up with the goods.

Years earlier she'd applied the term to Howard, whom I've already mentioned – our other next-door neighbour who dressed, whatever the weather, in the accepted filmic style of an intrepid explorer, wearing tan shirts with epaulettes and button-down pockets, sleeves rolled neatly above his elbows, khaki drill trousers and a heavy duty parka in winter. His shoes, an item we always intended to check out, but never got round to, we assumed to be of the desert boot variety. We assumed much about Howard: an important job in Birmingham Zoo, chief adviser to Jacques Cousteau, an Egyptologist perhaps. We glimpsed him hurrying in or out of his house at dusk or early morning. We could guarantee he was fleet of foot, even if we couldn't swear to his footwear.

Mum came into closer contact while spending quality time around the communal dustbins, Thursday evenings and Friday mornings, advising careless neighbours to "Please bag your rubbish, that's how disease spreads, encourages rats, undermines society as a whole."

She vouched that Howard was regular and tidy with his rubbish. 'Regular' in that he appeared, rubbish sacks in hand, just as the light was fading on Thursday evening and 'tidy' because his rubbish sacks were always firmly and neatly sealed with brown gummed tape and of the strongest garden refuse quality. As befitted a man who might spend most of his life travelling across the Serengeti, they were also khaki coloured.

However, he did have a surprising quantity of rubbish, considering he was a man alone, which backed up her theories of vampirism and nocturnal virgins brought home in the early hours.

"He entertains them first. Food and drink – hence the rubbish – dulls their senses, then..." She made a slashing motion across her neck.

I said, "Vampires bite, they don't use knives. And you reckon he settles them down to a three-course meal before having his wicked way? Sounds unlikely."

"It's very unlikely. Exactly my point. And men who cook are always reassuring."

"Men who cook are few and far between."

"Of course, the bags could contain dismembered bodies," she'd said thoughtfully, but she dismissed this theory the following week by testing the weight of Howard's rubbish sacks, after ensuring he'd set off for parts unknown down in the town centre.

"They're light. He could have minced the flesh and buried their bones." She watched me slyly to see if I'd take the bait. I didn't. This was in the golden days when Susan and I were still an item; I was reading our horoscopes and wondering at the coincidence that each morning they seemed to dovetail so uniquely.

> **Mine:** *Since your ruler Venus has just joined Mars, your powers of attraction are preternaturally heightened and someone not too far away finds you irresistible. Lay down your defences and accept the love fruits an admirer has to offer.*
> **Susan's:** *Now that Venus, the planet of love, has moved into your sign of Cancer, you feel ready to move heaven and earth to fulfil a loved one's dreams. Be adventurous; now is the time to experiment in affairs of the heart.*

I was musing on 'experiment' and what Susan's 'love fruits' might be, when I was vaguely aware of mum asking, "Why do men always wear orange foundation?"

I lowered the newspaper. "Pardon?"

"I'm asking you why men wear orange foundation."

"Apropos to what?"

"Apropos to Howard and that programme on Hollywood Men at the weekend."

"Does Howard wear make-up then?"

"I've just said he does."

"What do you think that's all about, then?"

Mum twitched with irritation. "You sound very common sometimes, Joan. It's Susan's influence. You used to speak like a perfect lady. It's 'all about' Howard wanting to look tanned all year round, I expect, but having nobody to tell him, he's missed the back of his neck."

"What about the virgins?"

"The virgins never see the back of his neck."

To cut a long story short, Howard looked like an intrepid explorer with an all-year tan but in actual fact he was just a chap who stayed at home and wore pan-stick: in other words, a fanny merchant.

I met Sandy in a pub in Kilburn on a boiling hot August afternoon in 1985. It was a straight pub and I'd bolted in to get out of the heat. I sat at a marble topped table feeling quite pleased with life; half of lager on my left, a packet of plain crisps still unopened on my right, in the middle, a paperback of short stories by Alice Walker I'd only just bought.

Sandy Banks made quite an entrance, filling the doorway with her tall shadow, dark against the bright summer street. She stepped forward and I could see her properly, tanned, in command, looking like the captain of any ship I'd care to be passenger on.

"That's the sort of old-fashioned lesbian I've been searching all my life for, or my name's not Joanie Littler," I thought.

I didn't for one minute think, "What's a woman doing in

a heavy serge blazer with all the buttons fastened when the temperature's nudging eighty?"

By this time, mum was a resident in Shepherd's Fennel Nursing Home, keeping her other old friend Mrs Scott company. Mrs Botolph had moved to a mansion flat in nearby Shoreham to keep them both company, and I'd moved to London.

I found a bedsitter on the first floor of a house near Dollis Hill tube station, which if anyone enquired was the Willesden/Kilburn borders – Dollis Hill sounding suburban and unexciting.

It suited me. My room was large and light. I viewed it in winter with a weak sun filtering through the window and imagined how it would seem when summer came. Outside was a leafless plane tree that reminded me of the two plane trees in the garden at home. A good omen. In summer, the room sizzled from early morning, retaining the heat through grey days of rain, but the tree was all I'd hoped for. Each night I fell asleep listening to the leaves rustling gently.

Financially, I was well off. I had half the money from the sale of the house in my building society account and almost immediately I began to get gardening work. It was a strange period of rest and solitude I'd never experienced before. I was living in London, but not yet a part of it. I wasn't lonely. On introspective days, I felt I was making ready to meet someone rather special. Without mum to take care of, I had more time to spend on myself; when I wasn't working I spent afternoons lying in parks, reading and sunbathing. I lost that indoor, pasty look I'd developed in Smallheath after Susan and I split up.

Sandy ordered a double gin and tonic, ice and lemon; a slight East End intonation to her voice. She paid with a twenty pound note taken off a wad of twenty pound notes. I said to myself, "An old-fashioned East End lesbian with her own money. Even better." I heard the rustle of silk between thighs and there by her side was a woman I gauged to be in her thirties. They kissed and hugged enthusiastically, giving me no chance to catch the eye of my chosen one, no chance for comparisons to be drawn between my, in those days, tanned athletic attractions, and her companion's only doll-like daintiness.

However... as the old-fashioned East End lesbian turned towards said companion with a tender smile, her gaze shifted, only for a second, but for that second she looked straight at me. She'd known I was there, watching her. She'd been assessing my interest in the mirror behind the bar.

I smiled.

She looked away, said, "Vodka and tonic," to the barman. They moved past me, carrying their drinks to the booths at the back of the pub, the fingers of her free left hand on the woman's spine gently steering her forward. Again as they passed my table, her head tilted a fraction in my direction and a look of acknowledged interest bounced between us.

I gave her ten minutes. I tried to concentrate on my book.

> *"Memories of years*
> *Unknowable women –*
> *sisters, spouses*
> *illusions of soul."*

I read that three times, forcing myself unsuccessfully to consider the importance of reading those words at that particular moment. Then I'd had enough. I drained my glass and took it back to the bar. I walked slowly, pleased with my cut-away white T-shirt, pale blue denim jeans, sawn off just above my knees. I was slim and brown; my hair, tied back with an ethnic scarf, swung heavily against my shoulder blades.

I leant thoughtfully on the bar, taking my time to fish out a fiver. It was better than a film. No sooner had my fiver fluttered in the breeze, and I'd murmured, "A dry white wine, please," in a perfectly modulated, slightly husky voice, than someone brushed against my bare arm and said, "Let me get this one for you, love."

"Thank you," I said – not a hint of surprise. Well done, Joanie, on that day.

"What's the book?" she asked, nodding towards my table.

"*In Love and Trouble*, by Alice Walker."

"Sounds good," she said, and "Same again," to the barman, and "See you around," to me.

I didn't see her again until a Saturday evening in late summer, although I looked. It was almost dark, nearly nine o'clock – light streamed across the forecourt from a car showroom window. There was a banner strung over the perspex facia, it said, 'Special Late Night Event at Simon Baldwin's – this week only.'

I was on the top deck of the Number 8 bus brooding on the changing seasons and how unappealing salad was once the weather cooled, when I spotted her. Even in the half-light I'd have recognised the gleam of her eight brass blazer buttons and the triangle of handkerchief in her breast pocket. She was leaning an immaculate elbow on the sunroof of a scarlet Ford Fiesta and chatting to a man in a checkered cap. By the time I'd hot-footed back from the next bus stop, he'd disappeared and an invisible someone was dimming the showroom lights. Sandy was still there, now taking a chamois leather lovingly over the humped bonnet of a two-tone Capri.

I shouted a "Hi there," and then, "The pub, Kilburn High Road, a couple of months ago. Remember?"

She hardly paused in her stroking, just nodded and gave me a slow, absent-minded smile.

"Lovely bit of bodywork, isn't it?" she said, "Only twenty-six thousand miles on the clock."

"It's a bit on the big side for me," I said, "I rather like that red Fiesta," and suddenly I had her complete attention. She turned towards me with a dazzling smile. Her eyes flicked over my face and body as if they held at least the attractions of a Special Edition Capri.

"Are you buying or window-shopping, sweetheart, because whatever your intentions, we are closing," she studied her watch, "now."

"I'll come back on Monday."

"Why don't you do that? Get here around lunchtime and I'll buy you a drink in the pub. OK?"

I walked the mile to Dollis Hill. I couldn't bear to sit still on a bus. I was too excited – I wanted to think with no distractions.

I met my landlady, Vi, in our communal hall. She was trying to fix a cushion to the seat of her bicycle. I said, "I have a date on Monday. It's rather serious actually. Been on the cards for some months, we've got tired of fighting our feelings."

"Oh yes, what's her name?" Vi asked, through a mouthful of sellotape.

I tapped my nose and said, "Ah ha – that's for me to know and you to find out, Vi, my dear."

I bought the red Fiesta. It took a good chunk of my savings as Sandy said I was a bad credit risk, being self-employed and no mortgage. It had to be cash or we were scuppered. She told me this over a second glass of ice-cold wine, (my round), and the 'we' made my cheeks glow. Immediately I saw us both as long-term: planning outings together, buying cars, houses, pedigree dogs. However, only I bought the red Fiesta and when my cheque for 'Simon Baldwin's – the Car Showroom' cleared, only then did Sandy Banks ask me out to dinner.

I'd never known anyone who dressed as formally as Sandy. It didn't worry me, not at first. I was intimidated but impressed. Her mother blue-bagged and spray-starched her shirts, ironed all her socks and underwear, every item of clothing – even the soft cashmere cardigans she wore at weekends had knife-edge creases. But her blazers... oh, her blazers.

She kept them, at least a dozen, in an especially built, ventilated cupboard in her spare bedroom.

"You got to keep 'em aired, Joan. Even with the dry-cleaning, they need to get air into the fabric."

I never asked why. There were blazers with military and nautical brass and silver buttons; double-breasted navy and black for work; a royal blue and a red for weekends and evenings; beige and cream summer weight for, well summer, and then there were the extra special ones that I only ever saw once, at the very beginning of our relationship. The ones she kept under tissue paper.

"My senior school blazer, Joan," she said reverentially, "Fifth and sixth year. Immaculate. Two of dad's: British Legion and Tottenham Hale Dominoes. Collectors' items."

There were others. I could go on.

Going out with Sandy, because we took some time to reach the staying-in phase, was like pursuing a highly desirable job – I had to prove myself worthy of her.

I endured three alternate Fridays being wined and dined in the drab emptiness of The Bombay Nights Bar and Brasserie, followed by what Sandy called her 'night-time snifter' at her local pub. I perched on a slippery plastic bar stool and rotated a single brandy in a bright, girlish fashion while Sandy and the barmaid discussed the latest advances in gabardine.

That third evening, when she ran me home in a borrowed black Volvo Estate bearing the memorable message 'Interested? Ring Simon Baldwin for your best deal' taped to the back window, she handed me one of her cream business cards and said, "That's my home address on the back. I thought coffee at my place, elevenish, Sunday morning. Leila always pops in. It'll give you both a chance to meet."

"Leila?" I queried.

"My mum."

"That's an unusual name."

"She's an unusual woman."

Sandy's flat was ideally positioned above a dry-cleaner's. Not only did she rent from them, she was also their best customer.

"This is lovely," I enthused, thanking god I was wearing new trainers. Soiled trainers were unimaginable in an environment of white leather, white walls and a carpet that was wall-to-wall virgin snow.

"Oh," I said breathlessly, and "How interesting." I stared intently at three sepia prints of vintage cars, then took my time reading the framed copy of Sandy's Advanced Driving Certificate, nodding sagely as if it was a well-known and dearly loved Shakespearean sonnet.

"Sit down, Joan," she said.

She looked wonderful. Brilliant white shirtsleeves rolled up to reveal tanned arms, collar open a couple of buttons to reveal tanned neck, fawn trousers with tan loafers, no socks, to reveal tanned ankles. I was overwhelmed by the wonder of her. I sat tensely forward on her long settee hoping I didn't look like someone inclined to slouch, while she sprawled casually next to me on the arm, apparently uncaring of her pristine upholstery. She was saying, "You see, Joan, before I do the business with anyone, I like Leila to have a shufty first."

"The business?"

"You know; sex, overnight stays."

And still I sat there. I forgave the 'business, sex, overnight stays'. Not even forgave, I was grateful she'd brought the subject up at last, in however an original form.

"So Leila's popping in with my ironing and she'll stay for about half an hour. OK?"

She tweaked a tendril of my hair. "Make yourself at home while I put the kettle on. Go on Joan, sit back, the cushions won't bite."

I sat back. What would this Leila be like? I imagined a big woman in a scrupulously clean flowered overall, two huge bags of ironing held in her ham-like, washday raw, red hands. Wispy grey hair in a bun, lots of black pins holding it in place. An adoring smile on her wide, honest face.

Leila let herself in with much noisy fumbling of the key.

"Hallo there," she shouted, "I'm not interrupting anything, am I?"

I heard the rustle of silk and polythene, then the half-open door behind me was barged wide with her hip and she came in sideways, trailing shirts in polythene covers from one hand, a large navy canvas bag in the other. She was doll-like and dainty; she was the woman I'd seen Sandy with in the pub, that first sighting. Immediately some sixth sense whispered that Leila would be a problem.

"Phew, I'm bushed," she said, laying the shirts carefully over the back of the sofa.

"I'm Joan," I said, leaping to my feet and holding out my hand. She looked at it dubiously, then gripped three of my fingers.

"Yes, I know you're Joan. She's never had a Joan before. I better get this lot put away before they crease."

She picked up the shirts and the bag; as she passed the kitchen door she called out, "Oi, oi, got a kiss for an ex-beauty queen?" and Sandy called back, "I'll be out in a minute, Leila, the pilot's on the blink again."

I returned to my place on the sofa to morosely consider Leila's unnatural youth and beauty.

"She's a wonder, isn't she?"

I started. Sandy had crept quietly up behind me bearing a polished chrome tray which she positioned carefully, dead centre of the glass coffee table.

"In what way?" I asked cautiously.

She looked offended. "Doing all my washing and ironing of course."

"Of course. She's very attractive as well."

"Isn't she? She's won titles."

She set out three square-shaped coasters with the favoured vintage car motif and I was reminded suddenly of Susan and the coincidence of twice being besotted with women who owned sets of coasters. I could live for years without sighting a coaster in anyone's home and then, there they were again, like a warning. One day, I might be mature enough to see a coaster and walk away; until then I'm possibly one of the few women in the world that can't look at a strange coaster without experiencing a tingle of anticipation.

The cupboard doors and drawers were banging merrily in the next room. I heard a window being opened.

"Stuffy in here, Sandy," Leila shouted from the bedroom.

"I don't like the street noise, mum," Sandy shouted back through a mouthful of plain digestive biscuit, "Are you coming in here, or what?"

"Coming, coming." Leila pirouetted back into the room. She'd removed her shoes and her pretty feet and ankles twinkled across the white carpet and deposited her, a graceful bundle, into one of the armchairs. I noticed her toes and fingernails were painted a pearly silver. She wore numerous silver bracelets, silver chains at her neck, a dusty brown silk dress.

"Say hello to Joan, Leila," Sandy said, offering her the plate of biscuits.

"We've said hello, haven't we, Joan?" She pouted at me for a second. "No ginger nuts, pet?" – back to Sandy.

"I'm off ginger nuts."

"She's off ginger nuts," she shrugged at me. "How's the pilot?"

"Fingers crossed."

"What do you do, Joan?"

"I'm a gardener."

"Oh yes," she helped herself to another biscuit, "Isn't that a very mucky job?"

"It can be. But it's only plants, soil and fertiliser. These days they're specially prepared; it's not as if fertiliser smells like horse manure."

"Fertiliser?" She wrinkled her nose as if horse manure was exactly what she could smell. "Well, keeps you out of trouble, doesn't it?" She and Sandy laughed fondly at each other.

After that small flurry of interest, for the most part they forgot my existence; so the pattern of our relationship was formed, with Leila always in the background.

Leila was 'modern'. Sandy's phrase. She possessed complete self-assurance, at least where Sandy was concerned. At any time of day or night, she let herself into Sandy's flat, walking into the bedroom, humming an unrecognisable tune and filling up the closets with an endless supply of clean shirts. Socks in this basket, knickers – colour-matched – in the chest of drawers by the window.

"Don't mind me," she'd say chirpily, not quite meeting our eyes, intent on the job in hand. Morning and she'd fling back the bedroom curtains so that we could see the passengers on the top deck of the bus. More absorbing for them, they could see us, sitting propped against Sandy's fawn velour headboard, sipping cups of tea and eating toast, thoughtfully provided by Leila who perched on the edge of the bed (Sandy's side), and told us what the state of play was like on the Victoria Line that morning. It was hard not to imagine she'd spent the night with us. That she'd crept in (Sandy's side) after I'd fallen asleep.

What did I get out of it? Why did I put up with her? These questions always come back to force one to wonder, when the heat dies out of a relationship, but even now, years later, I remember the potency of Sandy's kisses. She'd perfected a technique that made me put common sense and self-respect on hold for several months.

She used her kisses sparingly and to effect. Her lips were soft and gentle, becoming forceful and urgent. She had a way of holding me just above the elbows that promised passion; that promised visions of being roughly pressed against a hard orthopaedic mattress, head bounced repeatedly into a one hundred percent duck-down pillow.

In fact she kissed so well, so thoroughly, that for months this technique hid her lack of personal involvement. She was a woman who metaphorically wore her blazer even during moments of supposedly complete abandon. I began to feel that she was only revving up her forecourt performances, changing from persuasion, through tenderness to domination and finally victory. Her climax came each time I bought the performance. I could almost hear her slapping a sales sheet on to Simon Baldwin's desk and shouting, "Yes, yes, yes," pumping the air with a triumphant fist.

I told mum about her and to a smaller degree mentioned Leila. Mum hadn't understood, she wasn't good on romance. When I said, "But I'm certain Sandy loves me," she replied, "Doesn't sound too promising, Joan. I hope you haven't said. I'd be very disappointed if you have. I've never said that sort of thing to anyone."

But of course I had said, more than several times. Almost from the very beginning, I'd told Sandy how much I loved her. She'd said, "You're great too, Joan," and "We do have a good time, don't we?" and towards the end of our relation-ship, "Ta very much, Joan, nice of you to say so."

At Christmas, I'd intended to go down to mum's nursing home. It had several bedrooms where relations or close friends could stay overnight, or even a couple of days at a nominal fee. I didn't book a room. I kept putting it off, wait-ing to see what Sandy wanted to do.

"She'll surprise me," I thought, "There'll be tickets for the Swiss Alps, or Florida, or the Caribbean."

Sandy had travelled all over the world. She'd been a steward on a cruise ship before the motor business. "Got bored, darling, missed mum's cooking" – although I'd never known Leila tackle more than tinned soup and toast and marmalade.

In the week before Christmas my hopes became more modest, centring on my possible present, perhaps a dinner dance or a party. I wanted to see other women, to show Sandy off. I was tired of the unremitting Sandy, Leila and myself, the odd one out. I wanted a proper relationship, just the two of us, I was even thinking of putting my foot down.

Four days to go, in the afternoon she telephoned: "Come early, Joan. I've got the tree up, it looks terrific – I'd pick you up, only I'm waiting in for Leila."

"Don't worry," I said, "a walk will do me good."

"What about the Fiesta?"

"It keeps dying on me."

A pause from Sandy's end of the phone, then she said cautiously, "Sounds like you need a new battery."

"It's still under warranty. Should I bring it in to Simon Baldwin's?" I asked, not altogether disingenuously.

She hesitated, then said briskly, "Sorry Joan, jobsworth. Better take it into another garage. I can give you an address of one on the North Circular. Just mention my name."

I had a fair bit to mull over on my half-hour walk through cold light rain. I thought about Susan and the three Christmases I'd spent cheerfully richocheting up and down the road between our house and hers. I thought about festive parties I'd been to years ago with women I'd liked a lot but didn't love. I thought about mum with her glass of sherry that lasted the whole day who was bloody annoying but never boring... I reached no conclusions, but there was none of my breathless anticipation as I crossed Kilburn High Road towards Sandy's flat.

Sandy had left the sherry bottle on the coffee table with instructions for me to help myself while she heated up a boxed set of six mince pies. I sipped slowly and thoughtfully, watching Leila's red satin buttocks as she rummaged amongst the presents under the bright green plastic tree.

"That's a very nice outfit, Leila, is it new?"

"Christmas '79. Sandy bought it in a boutique in Bath. As a family we look after our clothes."

"Bully for you," I muttered. My presents for them were already beneath the tree: a pair of brown leather gloves with a fake mink trim at the wrists for Leila, and a miniature silver-plated Rolls Royce Phantom I'd found in a shop in Brighton for Sandy. I knew she'd love it once she'd organised a glass or perspex case to minimise problems with dust.

"Well, here's to Christmas," Sandy said cheerfully, coming in with her tray absolutely laden with a small bowl of peanuts, three mince pies and sherry glasses for herself and Leila.

"Christmas," Leila echoed, backing towards me dragging a shoebox wrapped in silver paper.

Sandy poured more sherry; we clinked our glasses, every-one smiling.

"One of our rituals," said Leila, "pre–going away drinkies with close friends. We like rituals, don't we, pet?"

"We love them," Sandy replied fondly.

"As in sherry and mince pies," Leila to me.

"Pie," I corrected her.

"What?" Sandy, a frown spoiling her smooth brow.

"There's only enough for one each."

"Plenty more in the kitchen." Sandy again.

"Only six in the packet." Me again.

"Well, how many do you want?" she snapped, her all-year tan beginning to redden at the neck.

"Dee-licious," said Leila, producing a pink tissue from her sleeve and wiping her hands and mouth as if she'd just devoured the main course of a medieval banquet, "Shall we give Joan her present?"

"Pre–going away where?" I asked.

"Edinburgh. Didn't I say? We always go to Edinburgh."

"We?"

Leila explained, "Sandy and I are spending Christmas in our usual hotel, but we won't be away more than a few days. In the meantime we want you to wear these and think of us. Don't we Sandy?"

Sandy, looking resentful still, muttered, "I'm sure I told you, we go every year, the Scots know how to celebrate festivals."

"Do they really?" I said, tearing the wrapping off the shoebox.

They'd bought me a pair of black velvet mules with an angora pompom on each. In the centre of the pompoms were small cats' heads with red jewel eyes.

"We chose them together," Leila said.

"You can keep them in my shoe drawer when you stay over, I don't mind," Sandy said, her good humour returning.

I took off my trainers, my woollen argyle socks, and slipped my plump pale feet into the mules. Then I teetered the length of the room, unsteady on the two-inch heels. As I neared the mirror, I saw my face, two inches higher up its surface than usual; my cheeks were bright red, my eyes glassy with tears or laughter – I couldn't decide which.

"Oh, don't take them off," Leila protested as I stepped out of them and reached for my socks.

"If you don't mind, I'd like to take them to show mum and Mrs Scott in the nursing home."

"Oh, isn't that sweet?" gushed Leila, "What's your mum buying you?"

"It'll probably be books, a friend does her shopping."

"Never mind. Old people always get it wrong, don't they?"

"We'll open your presents at the hotel, Joan," Sandy said gently. "You won't mind will you, only it's another one of our rituals, isn't it, Leila?"

"It is. Families are all about ritual, aren't they?" She smiled mistily and they both allowed that observation a thirty-second silence.

I watched them talking. I no longer listened or hoped to take part. Sandy relaxed, leant her head back on Leila's knee. I sat, cross-legged on the floor, a million miles away from them both, cradling my black velvet mules. After half an hour, they both went into the kitchen to heat up the remaining mince pies and make coffee. I called out to them, "I'll just pop my present in my rucksack."

I went into the hall. I heard Sandy come back into the room and put on a cassette. As I let myself quietly out on to the cold, dark stairs that led down to Sandy's street door, I heard the Ronettes begin to sing, warning that I had better watch out, better not cry and better not pout – then telling me why...

FIVE
1991
Being serious for a moment

It had been a year of cold, silent warfare; sad, droopy
Rachel versus myself – Joanie, the Jolly Jack Tar. I'd had that
nickname at school when I'd played a swash-buckling pirate
in the Christmas pantomime. In five years with Steff, I'd
reinvented myself, gone back to my earlier persona – bluff,
nautical sort of woman, even though I can't swim. Not like
Rachel – Steff says she swims like a fish. Pisces, so she would,
wouldn't she?

In all this time, I'd only met the aquatic Rachel once and
on that occasion I didn't take her for a swimmer or the
enemy. I thought I knew Steff's type and she wasn't it. Steff
liked to laugh and no one made her laugh like I did.

Steff's a serious woman; reader of heavy books in small
print with Notes and Appendices. She's not a Sandy or a
Susan, she's quiet and unobtrusive, but confident and warm
as well – I felt taken care of in a way I hadn't in the past. She
sharpened me up, presented me with options I didn't know
I had. Mum and me, we got by on our natural wit, an interest in films of any age or nationality, and what we'd gleaned

from all the many reference books we'd thumbed through together. We liked to think we had 'innate cunning' (Mum lifted that from *The World of Animals* 1954 – characteristic traits of the wolverine), which meant we could judge our audience and amend our material accordingly. We didn't need to read books; we knew the titles, authors, basic plot and whether it had been turned into a film; that was more than enough until Steff. She encouraged me to read – whole books, beginning to end and don't skip descriptions of countryside or sea – and, more importantly, she encouraged me to write.

"If you're going to write seriously, Joan, you'll need more than punchlines."

"Will I? I've always got by on punchlines."

"Getting by isn't good enough."

I'd never had anyone taking me seriously before. At first I felt awkward and self-conscious sitting on my own with a pad and pen trying to think up witty but erudite thoughts, but slowly, scraps of writing dropped randomly in a folder – purple plastic with green tassels, a thirty-fifth birthday present from Steff – began to add up. Writing was something I had, that I could do. That slowly filling file held out a hope that I wouldn't spend the rest of my life digging other people's gardens.

In return, I made Steff laugh. Sometimes till she cried, till she doubled over and yelled for me to 'please shut my mouth and go in another room'. She said she'd never laughed like that before, never seen the light or silly side of ordinary things.

Oh yes, there were moments when she was tempted by other women – a mobile face and a hard-luck story, some evidence of a sense of humour and Steff could be distracted for an hour, a day or two even – after all we'd been together several years, but no serious threat materialised. Those women weren't like me – no staying power. The years of dedication to being funny just weren't there and why should they be? I'd had to be funny. Therein lay my initial attraction; Joanie – funny but vulnerable, ensuring Steff came home at night, however scintillating the company.

Even recently I'd been able to tease out a smile, giving her my best ever rendition of 'chimpanzee grooms herself before going shopping'. I'd done that routine so many times before: on buses, in the park, at her brother's wedding. I was tempted at uncle's funeral, only it isn't easy balancing on one leg in six inches of mud. Not that I'm insensitive, but aunty had an aversion to uncle. She said he only had time for his nieces and daughter when their breasts sprouted. She wouldn't have minded at all. It would have diverted attention from her humming.

We met on a White City train. Later Steff said: a) she'd liked my chuckle, and b) I was the first *Reader's Digest* reader she'd ever seen under fifty.

If you're lucky, spending too much time with an elderly parent makes you sensitive and quirky rather than eccentric and cantankerous. Steff said I came into that first group. Apart from the quiz books, the crossword puzzle books, mum's flirtation with jigsaw puzzles until she lost the Queen Mother's head; the *Reader's Digest* was the favourite mum always fell back on, and I resorted to when nothing better was handy. Our spare room used to be crammed full of them, piled three-foot high and tied up with string – waiting. Mum was one of their earliest subscribers. A winner of a set of white, guest bedroom towels and a First Aid box. Never the cheque or the Ford Cortina.

The day I met Steff I was delivering a clutch of ancient *RD*s plus a box of New Berry Fruits minus two lime flavours to the hospital where mum was recovering – half of her colon had been removed at the weekend. Mum loved illness – even later on, when she played a more active part in it. I was pleased with the featured, true-life medical dramas I'd picked out for her: 'My triple bypass gave me the courage to love again' and 'Dead for five whole minutes – her prayers pulled me back'; the articles I always avoid. However, I did like the funny anecdotes of 'Life's Like That', and 'Humour in Uniform', so when Steff started chatting, I was chuckling away to myself. That first meeting we were friends, then more than friends. It was easy and natural. We agreed – the best way. Far better than meetings in pubs and clubs, artificial parties, dressed up and trying to impress with clever conversation.

So, where did she meet Rachel? At a party. Their eyes met across a crowded room. "Just like the song," Steff said – too corny for me to ever forget. And true to dear old Oscar Hammerstein's lyrics, Rachel flew to Steff's side and made her her own, and now all through their lives – and God please make those as short as possible – they won't dream all alone and never mind the poor sod who will.

And where was I, while this momentous meeting was taking place? In the kitchen presiding over the drinks, where anybody who's any fun congregates, and as always fancying myself the life and soul of the party.

Once or twice, I looked into the sitting room to check Steff was all right. She was sitting on the floor listening to a serious-looking soul with long hair and glasses who was mumbling earnestly in response to Steff's head-nodding.

I shouted from the doorway, "Don't be a stranger," "Life is a cabaret old chum," and "Party, party," but Steff just waved her glass at me with an absent smile. I imagined she was bored stiff, but what could I do? I was not my lover's keeper.

Back in the kitchen, I collared Penny, one of the first friends I'd made after the Sandy Banks fiasco.

"Who's the woman with the long blonde hair, and is it natural?"

Penny prised herself free from her companion, who continued to stroke her arm as if it was a dearly beloved pet.

"That will be Rachel, and yes it is natural. Amazing colour."

"Amazing," I rumpled my own rich brown tresses with burgundy highlights.

"She's extremely intelligent… No more, darling" – this to the woman grooming her arm. "A psychotherapist. Published two reference books in America – the last word on something reproductive, and a book out here in the spring called *The Mother–Daughter Orgasm*."

"You seem to know a lot about her."

"I do. We went out together for a week, but she dispensed with my services. Said she'd mistaken me for a Penny Kroestler, some authority on menopausal behavioural problems."

"Poor Steff. I bet she's bored."

"Oh I don't know. Rachel's got great tits."

As much as I liked and respected Penny, sometimes she disappointed me. I was tempted to say, "If great tits are all that's required to be popular, I should have had much better luck with women than I have had." Instead I smirked and shrugged and muttered, "Yeah, see what you mean, Pen," but Penny's attention was elsewhere, nuzzling her friend's denim jacket.

In the car going home, I asked, "Was Rachel as dreary as she looked?"

"She wasn't dreary at all. Did you get a chance to speak to her?"

"That would have been difficult, she'd glued herself to you for the evening. Penny told me her name – said they'd gone out for a week, but Rachel found her a little too low-brow."

"Penny can be obtuse."

"Can she? That's a bit hard on her. Give me Penny any day of the week. I couldn't bear to be mumbled to death by that droopy New Age hippy."

"Actually Joan, she was really nice."

"Really nice," I mimicked drunkenly. "For 'nice', read bloody, bum-numbingly boring. You'd never get a word in with that one."

"Don't be nasty, Joan. I said nice and I meant it. I wouldn't mind asking her to dinner, she was a very interesting woman, unfortunately she's also had a very hard life."

"No, no. Please spare me from interesting women with hard lives. They're taking over the world. Oh god, pins and needles in my chest, aaahh…" I pretended to slump unconscious over the steering wheel and the car swerved into the middle of the road.

Steff steered with one hand, she was laughing.

"You're a hard bitch, Joan. Stop mucking about and drive this car."

I was glad I'd made her laugh and hopefully forget Rachel and dinner, but I didn't like her thinking me a 'hard bitch'. It hurt. I should have said something then and there only it didn't seem important enough to precipitate a row. I hated rows. We rarely had them. I associated them with endings, or beginnings of endings, and anyway, I had the complacency of a successful five-year relationship at my back, a mortgage in both our names. Not for one moment could I imagine that intense little shadow-woman dislodging it.

In retrospect, I've wondered if I could have headed Rachel off; asked her to dinner, made a friend of her, made it difficult for her to cold-bloodedly go behind my back and start an affair with Steff.

Mum said, "It takes two to tango," when I visited her in the nursing home. "Mrs Botolph's grandson-in-law's run off with a snooker player."

"What? He's gone off with a man. Good old Ray. One in the eye for po-faced Gemma."

"Not another man. Her name's Peggy and she's very big in Ladies' Tournaments. Very big. Mrs Botolph says she has to wear specially made brassieres to stop her bosoms rubbing on the felt."

"How did Mrs Botolph come by that piece of information?"

"Ray told Gemma, the night before he left. He said Peggy needed him to take care of little things like that."

"Could we come back to my problems, mum?"

"If we must," she sighed.

They met again – Rachel and Steff, not Peggy and Ray – at a three-day seminar. It was inevitable, in the stars, apparently. They talked all afternoon and evening, that first day – it was easier to continue talking in bed.

"And that's all we did – just talk," Steff said. "It wasn't till the last night when there was a get-together."

"A get-together? Do you mean a party? Must make a note for mum, don't think that's in her thesaurus."

Steff, being Steff, was scrupulously honest. From the first I was kept informed. I was her good friend; had I not also been her lover, I think she'd have liked to share more of her soul-searching with me. I told myself to stick it out, wait for boredom to set in, tried sympathy and understanding, then recriminations, all those 'you owe me' and 'what I've done for you'. I fought hard, as I'd never done for anyone in the past.

Strange how all our friends became Steff's friends. At first they stood on the sidelines, but eventually they came down in favour of the romantic lovers rather than Joanie, the Jolly Jack Tar.

After that one evening at the party, I didn't see Rachel again, but my imagination added to the vague impression I had of her. Her hair became ever lighter and silkier, mermaid's hair; there were no lines on her face, only thoughtful planes and angles. Even her voice changed. No longer monotonous, I heard it, low and musical, each word clever and worth Steff listening to. And as Rachel changed, so did I. Some of my humour crept away and I saw it gathering quietly behind Rachel's eyes, so that sometimes she made Steff laugh and that laughter was more precious for its rarity.

We sat in the garden: Steff and I and Edith Piaf, our joint cat – now mine alone. The apples were turning from green to red. It was warm with an erratic sun. All day we'd lived through a peaceful truce. Then out it came, as if someone had twisted a key at the back of my head. My mouth opened and I asked bluntly, "What's sex like between you two, then?"

"I don't want to talk about it."

"But just to satisfy me. One phrase. A little slice of heaven. Light blue touchpaper and stand well back. Come on Steff, an adjective, maybe two. Hot, steamy, you name it, we've done it. It's not much to ask. I'm the one left with only the cat for company."

"Gentle, that's how it is with Rachel. Satisfied?" She stood up and walked back into the house. I marched in after her.

"Don't you walk away from me," I bawled, following her down the hall into the front room.

"Joan, go away. I don't want to argue."

I could see the pity in her eyes, hear the sorrow in her voice. I hated them. Sorrow and pity; twin kisses of death. For once, I tried to change the tempo, push her into fighting back.

"Gentle, how pathetic," I sneered. "What do you do in bed, kiss 'night-night', and get off to sleep?"

"You're being silly."

"And of course Rachel's never silly. I bet she doesn't make you laugh like I did."

"No Joanie, she doesn't."

"Well then," I said.

"Laughter's not everything."

Habit I suppose, I nearly said, "Laughter's the best medicine." I stopped myself and muttered, "It's a lot."

Steff sat down on the sofa and closed her eyes. Very tiredly she said, "It is better to be drunk with loss and beat the ground than to let the deeper things escape."

"Says who?"

"Ivy Compton-Burnett."

"Well, what a miserable old bag she must have been to live with," I shouted.

"Those are very special words, they sum up Rachel's approach to life. She had them framed and hung in her kitchen. That's where she sits and thinks when life is difficult."

In my kitchen, I have a pinboard covered with old but cheering postcards I've collected or been sent by friends. Simple words: "Walk a mile in another woman's moccassins," "Even daisies need a shower of rain," "Behind every successful woman is a cat with an empty dish." No Ivy Compton-Burnett.

It's dark. I haven't switched on a light. I wouldn't want Edith Piaf to see the state of my face at the moment. She's a sensitive cat. I've almost finished a bottle of Bulgarian Country. Steff and I always bought it because it's cheap enough to have every evening. We decanted it before dinner into the crystal carafe we bought in the antique market at Camden Passage. Just one of the many little affectations couples are so proud of. Tenuous as laughter and shared experiences, yet still you imagine each one adds another fibre to the rope that binds you both together. Not so.

SIX
1994
No more Ms Nice Woman

The invitation was on heavy cream card. It had a border of holly, mistletoe and fir boughs drawn with a scratchy pen, which I immediately recognised to be artistic rather than for want of a new biro. Beneath "To Joanie and friend" was a paragraph of type in Garamond Italic which was so fine as to be almost impossible to decipher. I rested the card between Edith Piaf's ears and read:

An evening of wassailling, spiced beer and mulled wine.
Join us.
Bring holly, bring greenings [Greenings?] *and let us*
ceremoniously and in true sisterly spirit watch them burn.
Let the ash of the old replenish the dormant new.
As the Magi welcomed the baby Jesus, so your babies
and children are also welcome. Bring a bottle.
Love Penny and Jenny

Penny had been with Jenny just over two years. They both worked in computer graphics which enabled them to have a mortgage on a double-fronted house in Islington with multiple original features, while I still lived in my unmodernised two-bedroomed terrace in Stoke Newington with paraffin heaters for warmth, and two pairs of socks and a woolly hat to wear in bed.

I mused a little, warming my hands against Edith's fur. I wondered if I'd find a welcome there for her. If I located some swaddling rags. There must be something suitable on my wardrobe floor. I saw myself carrying her into their house: a pale pink crocheted shawl wrapped around her head, little paws folded over each other, encased in ribboned mittens. Me, bustling importantly through the party crush, demanding access to a smokeproof, noiseless room where I could feed her without personal stress to either mother or cat. If only Edith was more pliable, but she could be an ornery devil.

"I can't leave that lamp on all evening, Edith," I said severely, "It's a fire hazard."

She yawned and curled prawnlike around its base.

"If you go up in smoke, don't blame me. My manuscript shan't perish with you."

I gathered up my papers – hardly a manuscript – and took them out to the kitchen

This was one of my several nightly rituals, the placing of anything of value into a small tin trunk by the kitchen door; I'd long since outgrown the purple plastic file Steff had given me. A burglar would have been unimpressed with my secondary, sellotaped spectacles, a photograph album of Steff and myself in happier times and two exercise books of finished and unfinished jokes.

I feared a fire, and for some reason I always imagined it would be started by Edith in the front room. I was almost resigned to it. She was the sort of cat to catch fire. She trod on hot hotplates, left her tail resting on glowing hundred-watt light bulbs, sniffed lighted candles, she was a silly cat. So I kept my treasures by the back door, easy to grab them and go should the occasion arise.

The day of the party was freezing. It was only the sixth of January – Epiphany. I wondered if Penny and Jenny had noticed it was Epiphany in their 'A hundred stylish facts for each day' diaries, checked it out in the Bible, then without exchanging a word on the subject, both heard their friends' voices cooing over such unfailing originality. They wouldn't have heard mine.

I hadn't seen them since the previous autumn and I still bore a grudge. In fact I shouldn't have been going at all, except as I explained to Edith, "Beggars can't be choosers." This was my first social invitation in over two years. The last time I'd been out in the evening had been to see an exhibition of paintings depicting the sequential change in the vagina during childbirth. My ex-friend Petra had thought it would cheer me up after Steff walked out. I still had a book of postcards from the exhibition, somewhere. I'd intended sending the happy couple, i.e. Rachel and Steff, one a month after the dust had settled with "You die tonight" scrawled on the back.

The previous autumn, I'd had a bumper crop of apples. I'd made myself apple pie and apple crumble, stewed apple and baked apple, but it was no fun eating such quantities on my own. I could do it. It was enjoyable, particularly with tinned custard and sugar, only the scraped dishes were a nasty reminder that no one should eat that much at one sitting, and if they did, somewhere there was a problem.

So I filled two large carrier bags with apples and took them round to Jenny and Penny who I hadn't seen for ages. I knew they had a garden. We'd all been sent copies of the estate agent details when they'd moved out of Hackney. "Got out of Hackney," Penny had said on the phone at the time in a rather snobbish manner. But it was a sunny day, perfect for sitting in someone's else's garden and having them make me a cup of tea, or better still pouring me a sherry, so I set off.

Their house was approximately two miles away. For some reason I thought that between the start and the finish of my virtuous trek, the three stone in extra weight that I'd put on would vanish and I'd arrive a gracefully endowed woman with a prettily flushed face.

I could hear the murmur of happy voices from their back garden as I passed by their high wooden fence and I began to smile. As I rounded the corner and pushed open the wrought-iron gate, my smile had become loud, tuneful humming. I waited expectantly on their elaborately tiled doorstep, having pressed the doorbell with my forehead, my hands being engaged with the carrier bags. My humming had taken shape and I was now muttering, "This is my lovely day, this is the day I will remember the day I'm dying. All happiness must stray…"

A curtain twitched and I paused to smile. I heard Jenny say, "Oh damn it, who the hell's that?"

I could see her outline coming towards me, through the stained glass. The door half opened.

"Yes?" she snapped, a heavy frown showing through her fringe. I held out my carrier bags, waiting for a confident 'Hi there' or 'Surprise, surprise' to slip with cheerful carelessness from my mouth.

"I'm sorry. I can't buy anything. We've no change in the house."

She turned to close the door.

"Jenny, it's me," I said.

Her irritation vanished – not to pleasure, to embarrassment.

"Good god, Joan, I hardly recognised you."

"It's been a long time," I muttered defensively. "I was in the area visiting friends and I thought I'd pop by with some apples for you both." I put the bags down heavily inside the doorway; she grabbed them up and I noticed she was holding the door in its half-open position with her foot.

"Look Joan, I'm sorry," her voice dropped to a stage whisper, "Steff and Rachel here. It's a bit tricky."

"Oh, I wasn't stopping," I said quickly, "Just passing. Nice to see you. Love to Penny."

"And it's lovely to see you too. Love to er…"

"Edith?" I said with mild sarcasm – lost on Jenny of course.

"Yes, love to Edith."

Now, getting dressed for the evening's festivities, I mused over 'Joanie and friend'. That was it, I nodded to my bulky reflection. They thought Edith was my girlfriend. But wouldn't Steff have said? Whatever, I was sure that was the reason for my invitation. "At last Joan's found herself a girl-friend, now we can ask her over."

Couples hate singles. If they're attractive and confident they're a threat; shy and miserable and they're a constant blot on everyone's high spirits. A dark and desperate shadow standing hopefully in corners, or worse, in the middle of the room. Then if they drink too much they start crying or are sick, or overdose on antibiotics found in their hostess's bathroom cabinet.

That was how I'd wrongly imagined Rachel when I'd first seen her. The type of woman who arrived early at parties to prepare fifty potatoes for baking, chop enough salad to feed five thousand and start the barbecue while her hostess was still experiencing orgasms upstairs in the bathroom, and insisting between times that the helpers use the outside loo.

"This won't do, Joanie," I told my reflection, "tonight will not be a disaster, women will fall at your feet."

I pulled a large woollen hat over my blue fleck scull cap, zipped up my maroon padded jacket and pinned my lucky silver dolphin brooch to my breast. My reflection spilled generously over the mirror's pine frame.

"Don't wait up, dear," I called cheerily to Edith, as I clumped heavily down the hall.

In the off-licence I resisted the cheap bottle of Pink Lady and stuck with Bulgarian Chardonnay.

"Cheap but reliable, as the showgirl said to the bishop," I murmured, then gave myself a serious warning. "There is no need to be funny, Joan. Limit yourself to pleasantries. Do not make Baby Jesus jokes."

Their side gate was open and strung with white fairy lights, so in I went. The garden was smaller than I'd imagined but immaculate. I wondered at the bonfire being sited in the middle of the lawn but later heard Penny say to someone, "The lawn's going next weekend. We're enlarging our patio area. It's necessary now with the increase in our social circle."

It seemed fitting that I didn't own a patio area.

There were about twenty women and half a dozen young children. I knew several of the women, but not by name, and it wasn't a party where the hostesses made introductions. I stood at the edge of the bonfire stamping my feet in what I hoped was an enthusiastic and congenial manner. After a minute of this, I riffled through my off-licence carrier bag for the small twigs of 'greenings' I'd removed from a neighbour's overhanging laurel bush. I tossed them on the fire, nodding and smiling festively. Immediately the flames that had been dancing merrily skywards turned to hissing grey smoke and began to billow towards the open French windows. I felt quite sick. Not about the smoke, only suddenly I'd seen Steff and Rachel on the other side of the bonfire. Between them, holding on to their hands, was a little girl well wrapped against the cold. She was about three years old.

Steff was looking straight at me, grinning in a pleased, hopeful way. I felt so gratified that she was actually pleased to see me. I pushed aside the niggle that she'd been pleased not to see me for nearly three years. I wasn't ready for them yet – I needed a drink. I held up a gloved hand in salute, smiled, made a drinking gesture and headed for the garden table where Jenny was dispensing mulled wine from a large, steaming saucepan.

"Joan, I'm glad you could make it."

"Shall I take my bottle of wine into the kitchen?" I asked.

"Just leave it under this table. I don't want people traipsing mud into the house."

"Traipsing's an old-fashioned sort of word, Jen," I said cheerily.

"Perhaps I'm an old-fashioned sort of woman. I'm sure Pen has an opinion on that. Mulled wine?"

"Could I try the spiced beer?"

"'Fraid not. Pen's department and it just hasn't materialised. Sorry."

"Mulled wine it is, then."

She half filled a plastic cup and handed it to me.

"You couldn't fill it up, could you? Save me a trek back for more, traipsing mud on to the patio, etc."

"Very amusing. Is Freda with you?"

"Freda?"

"Didn't you say you were with a Freda?"

"Oh Freda. Yes," I nodded, "How were the apples?"

"Delicious. We sent Rachel off with a bag. You didn't mind, did you? She's a wonderful pastry cook."

Jenny began to fill another cup. Freda's cup.

"Actually Freda's more involved in pasta, although she can turn her hand to most matters culinary, hence my added weight." I tried out a modest yet complacent smile before turning on my heel, my cups balanced at ear level, which I imagined was a jaunty way to carry cups at a party. I did feel jaunty, from the moment I'd gone along with the Freda misunderstanding.

As I walked back across the frosty grass towards Steff and Rachel I knew that somewhere on the South Coast, Freda, my soulmate, was enduring a loving but tedious evening with her elderly parents.

I nodded to faintly familiar faces, said, "Hi, how are you. Nice to see you again," and "Must have a chat in a minute." Suddenly my weight was an asset. My body, my prow-like breasts enhanced by the padding of my jacket, was parting the small crowd. I beamed, a wide rapturous beam, and shouted from some yards away, "Steff, Rachel, it's lovely to see you," as if I'd only just spotted them.

I leant forward and kissed the air between their heads; the child stepped backwards with a cry of alarm.

"It's all right, darling," Rachel said, "This is Joan, an old friend."

Steff glanced quickly at me, but my beam stayed in place, only my voice grew louder, "And what's your name, little girl?" I boomed. She began to cry and buried her face in Rachel's coat.

"I'll take her inside for a few minutes, she's over-excited."

Steff and I watched them go. I drained my plastic cup and tossed it on to the bonfire. It hit the embers and they flared into life, then it buckled blackly and the flames died down.

"I'm sorry if I frightened her, I'm not used to children. Is she yours?"

"Rachel's her physical mother, but we're co-parenting."

"Gosh," I said inanely, for some reason thinking wistfully of Edith. "What's her name?"

"You'll laugh."

"Try me."

"Persephone."

I didn't laugh. I nodded sagely, "And do you call her that all the time?"

"Yes."

"Wasn't she raped and pillaged by Hades or was that someone else?"

"Are you making a critical judgement on our choice, Joan?"

"Does that mean I'm not allowed to?"

"Look, let's not argue." Steff paused, then said, "It's good news about Freda."

"Is it?"

"Well yes, you're not single any more. That's good, isn't

it? You always liked being part of a couple."

It was as if the years had rolled back and it was the day Steff left me, only I wasn't sad and devastated any more, I was angry. I finished off my wine and concentrated on the inside of my empty cup.

"Freda has her life, people change. I've changed. These days I value my own space. She lives on the coast, near mum's nursing home, pops in and sees her for me."

My spirits began to rally as the image of Freda returned. "She has a bungalow quite near the sea. Works part-time in a market garden, we have a lot in common."

I smiled mistily into the darkness, musing at the wonder of our many common meeting points.

"And are you really happy, Joan?"

That has to be one of the nastiest, most undermining questions. If one is happy, it's enough to make you reconsider and find life wanting, and if you're not – if like me, you're some fool trying to give a fair impression of cheerfulness and get through an evening while hanging on to a remnant of self-respect – it knocks tears up and into your eyes.

"I've never been happier," I said solemnly as if I'd given my state of happiness considerable thought, "And yourself?"

"I don't think I could say I'm happy all the time, but then Rachel and I don't value it as you do."

Wrongfooted again. "Well I feel sorry for you both," I said unpleasantly.

Steff patted my arm and said, "I really didn't mean that

to be critical in any way of your life. Live and let live, you know me, Joanie?"

"Do I? Well that's all right then. As long as I know you. By the way, just who are you? Excuse me, I must eat, drink and be merry. Know thy priorities." I began to move away from her.

"Will you and Freda come to dinner one evening?" she persisted.

"No, we will not. I couldn't bear to see Freda's happiness quotient reduced by the two of you, with your miserable, self-righteous earnestness. I couldn't do it to her. I like to see Freda smile. Remember Steff, what it is to smile and laugh without stopping to think whether you should or not? Remember, eh?"

I was almost jumping up and down with the luxurious fullness of my words. They streamed out in a torrent of half-good-natured insults. Steff pushed past me and headed for the French windows.

"Don't traipse mud into the house," I roared into the complete silence that had fallen around me.

Later I discussed the Freda situation with Edith. We sat together in the kitchen, she lapping tepid milk from a saucer, me drinking a mug of sugary hot chocolate.

"So you see, Edith, just supposing I continue with this and other people want to meet her, I'll be forced to fabricate a life, possibly to move out of London to avoid discovery, even a fake suicide may be on the cards. What should I do?"

Edith licked her whiskers, attended to her paws, then padded off towards my bedroom.

Somewhere on the South Coast, Freda began washing up her parents' Complan mugs. She took a pink hot-water bottle from a hook behind the larder door, and filled it with recently boiled water. Hugging it against her stomach, she leant back against their old chipped but scrupulously clean butler's sink and thought of Joanie.

She considered ringing her from the telephone in the hall, but it was cold out there, her feet were bare; mum and dad, bless them, might wake up. She'd ring when she got back to the bungalow in the morning.

I finished writing. I'd find a photograph in one of mum's old magazines, better still a line drawing, harder to trace. Get it reproduced – I knew a shop. "So romantic. She has one of me of course. An artist friend in Littlehampton did them. It's very like her."

I put the piece of paper in my trunk by the kitchen door and followed Edith up to bed.

TAPE 3

Q: Joan, could we talk a little about close personal relationships?

Joan: Yours or mine?

Q: Ha-ha. Very funny. Would you call yourself promiscuous or experimental?

Joan: One year I did resolve to be promiscuous; I'd respond to any woman who gave me a kind smile.

Q: And?

Joan: Nobody gave me a kind smile that year.

Q: So, we've reached 1994 and by this time you are…

Joan: Twenty-two.

Q: Thirty-nine. It seems to me that most of your sexually active life had been spent in monogamous relationships – fairly serious on your part.

Joan: I think the other people were serious at first – they just didn't have my staying power.

Q: But were they as serious?

Joan: Well, perhaps not. Perhaps they saw me as merely the hors d'oeuvre before their main meal.

Q: And you saw them as your main meal?

Joan: That's not the best way of describing my feelings. I'd rather think I was an optimist who entered each relationship with the hope that it would be lasting. OK, I wasn't promiscuous, I wasn't experimental, but I was caring and funny. There's not that many funny women around, whereas you'll find dozens being promiscuous and experimental.

Q: You sound annoyed.

Joan: I don't like being undervalued – I never did. [Pause] Anyway, I had many, many infatuations in-between times.

Q: Which led on to…

Joan: Homebase, and me purchasing their entire stock of Leyland Cypress, and further led to a forest of Leyland Cypress appearing overnight in a field on the outskirts of Bromsgrove.

Q: That would have been Jennifer in gardening?

Joan: Management had overstocked and she was very persuasive.

Q: To cut several long stories short…

Joan: You're getting bored, aren't you?

Q: Not at all; but we're already halfway through the session and I really want to get on to the Freda/Freddy dilemma.

PART TWO

SEVEN
1994
The Freda/Freddy dilemma

Waking up with a slight hangover, the morning after Jenny's and Penny's Twelfth Night Party, I dismissed Freda as a really bad idea. From the euphoria of the night before when she'd been a woman of flesh and blood and living in Littlehampton, she was now a grey indistinct figure walking away from me along an empty rainswept seafront. No longer a barefooted beauty in a thin nightdress, naked underneath and simmering with sexual invitation, no longer strong-hipped and leaning on a weathered five-bar gate, no longer did tanned toes splay in wet morning grass. Standing at my front window gearing myself up to catch the bus for Islington to unblock a customer's drain, all I could see was drab Freda in sensible shoes and too much tweed. I didn't like her shopping bag either – neatly packed with medicine, elastic bandages and foot plasters. A large ugly purse with money-off vouchers, a leaflet offering two tubes of toothpaste for the price of one and a worn compartment bulging with lowly denominated coins.

At the bus stop I allowed myself to think of Steff and

Rachel. There of course my dissatisfaction lay. However smug and dull and self-righteous they had seemed, theirs was a family unit. They'd looked happy until my boisterous intervention. They'd also looked well fed and smartly dressed in an effortless way only other people manage for bonfires in Islington. And the little girl, Persephone, she was probably a very dear little girl, quite unaffected by her name.

I was envious, and mythical Freda was worse than inadequate. I hadn't even succeeded in imagining somebody that anyone would be impressed with; I had made Freda into an extension of myself – feminine and put upon, untended and going to seed. In the bleak morning light, I had no intention of ever using Freda again – but just supposing I did, she would need more thought. Ailing parents would do, but she must have a car and work out at the gym; seaside, so a strong swimmer, possibly some life-saving certificates. Junior South East Champion in her youth but no time to pursue it now – too busy with the market garden and 'ma' and 'pa'. Extensive notes would be needed. Had I undermined my story already? I'd been a little careless describing her. I'd rather she wasn't such a whizz at pasta, better a magician with a jigsaw – and Freddy. That would be more appropriate. Freddy, yes I liked that.

I was in no mood for Mrs Jennings querying twenty pounds for clearing her drain when I arrived, before even offering me a mug of tea or coffee. She was loaded. She had a large three-storey house with attractively converted basement – window-boxes on every sill. I'd planted them up in the autumn with heathers, spring bulbs and a central variegated hebe. She was one of my regulars which was the only reason I'd agreed on the drain. Spring and autumn I cleared and planted, then fortnightly maintenance during the summer. Her son, Sam, mowed her lawn. He called it 'my mother's lawn' as if it were some special attribute that added not only the value of the property but also the value of his mother. I considered both overpriced.

"It's more expensive than having the whole garden done," she complained, standing several feet away from me, tapping her exquisite leather shoes on the frozen York-stone slabs, a fur coat draped over her shoulders.

"It's messy work, Mrs Jennings, and it's below freezing."

"Is it?" She looked up at the sky doubtfully. "Surely not?"

We had a moment's standoff; her small red mouth grew more pinched and a little frown appeared on her well-powdered forehead.

"It's up to you," I said with a reasonable smile and the hint of a shuffle to imply I could just as soon get off home.

"Oh very well, but I don't know what Sam will say."

"I expect he'll be very pleased to have it done."

"Mmmm," she said in an insincere, sadly disappointed with me, manner.

The drain took the best part of two hours to unblock. There was half an inch of dirty ice over the blockage, which was a very old, dead pigeon, almost skeletal but with most of its feathers still intact.

I said, "This must have been stuck down there for

months, Mrs Jennings."

"Well, the water has been rather sluggish. Sam poked around with a peastick and it improved for a day or two."

She was peering at me from the half-open kitchen door. I noticed she was now wearing her fur coat properly, buttons done up to her neck and also soft leather gloves – obviously on her way out.

"I'm just finishing now, Mrs Jennings, if we could settle up."

"Did it take as long as you thought? It seems you've been very quick."

"Two hours almost. I'm sorry, it has to be twenty."

"I don't know if I've any change in the house."

"I think I can change a fifty," I said, which was a lie, but I knew she had the money.

She disappeared and the door closed. Five minutes later she leant a small cream envelope with 'Joan' written on the front against a large, terracotta pot. "Just a little something extra," she simpered, "I'm off now, make sure the back gate's secure."

I finished shovelling black mud into a plastic sack and rinsed my hands under the outside tap. The 'little extra' was a Christmas card, too small for the envelope; the twenty tucked inside. "Merry Christmas and a Happy New Year. All the best from Mrs Jennings." She'd added 'belated' between 'Merry' and 'Christmas'. I put the money in my back pocket and let myself out into the alley that ran between the houses. I dropped the card in the first litterbin I came to on my way to the bus stop.

***

It was an afternoon for thinking. Either that or falling asleep on the settee with Edith, who looked a companionable cat, stretched out amongst the cushions. I opted for thought and sat down at my desk and began to doodle a cobweb in the margin of my pad. I put my head down on the desk and almost nodded off; stood up abruptly and went out into the kitchen.

Back again with a cup of tea – I started a fresh sheet of paper. I wrote down all the years in my life that had ever meant anything to me. More paper for the individual years to chart important events: going back to Smallheath from London, meeting Susan, breaking up with Susan, meeting Steff, breaking up with Steff, the train journey home after leaving mum behind at Shepherd's Fennel Nursing Home.

I went into more detail. Stopped myself from going into too much detail, my desk and floor were swamped with pieces of paper. I used red, blue and black biros, to emphasise order of importance. Finally I reached a conclusion: I had wasted most of my life, particularly during periods of happiness. At these points, the real me had disappeared underground while I thought I supported and sustained someone, although it was now apparent that my support and sustenance hadn't necessarily been welcome.

The years in between were inactive on my part. I'd been mildly depressed, waiting for somebody or an event to sweep me forward. I knew it all, deep down; this was the first time I'd seen my life written out in red, blue and black. It was no fairytale and I wasn't about to change, jump up from my chair and shout, "Eureka Edith, the pursuit of happiness must be set aside in the search for 'self'."

I gave in. Thoughts like these were exhausting. I nudged Edith aside and lay down on the settee, waking into semi-darkness, the room lit by the street light. I had no idea what time it was; the backs of my thighs where Edith had slept felt cold. The clock ticked and the sound of traffic on the road outside was muffled. I turned my head, cheeks still pressed into the warmth of the cushion. It was snowing heavily, the light immediately outside my house was like a shaky yellow reflection on a dark pond.

Quite cheerfully I thought, "I'm forty. I'm poor, getting older, uglier, fatter. I'm alone, pathetic, with only a cat for company." Then I thought, "I do have my own house, even if it is cold and bare. I have this settee and these cushions, a talent for gardening and I can be amusing. I made Steff and Susan laugh which wasn't easy, and years and years ago from six to sixteen…" At this point I lost my train of thought and forced myself to focus on mum by way of a distraction. I almost got up and rang her at the nursing home.

Before she became ill, she'd always made people laugh. Thoughtlessly – not like I did, to try and ensure a welcome. She'd never been grateful when people responded with more than just laughter. I remembered her complaining to me, after several visitors had turned up around teatime and then refused to budge, "Why can't they go home and stay home?"

"You were so amusing the other week, they can't get

enough of you; anyway I expect they imagined you liked them."

"I did last week, after several sherries. I like most people after a couple of drinks. I wasn't committing myself to a lifetime's friendship."

"Well they weren't to know that, were they? If you hang on to someone's arm and tell them they remind you of William Holden in *Bridge on the River Kwai*, they'll be flattered."

"I wouldn't want William Holden cluttering up the sitting room at teatime, I like to watch the six o'clock news."

I fed Edith who was crouched on the kitchen table staring at a cupboard. It was only half past seven. I took cake and my file, ambitiously labelled 'Comedy Routines', to bed with me.

I allowed myself half an hour of daydreams. My ideas were vague but grand. I was a famous comedienne, the funniest woman in Britain. Winning Perrier Awards, the star attraction at the Edinburgh Festival. Of course, I'd be unable to use public transport because of hysterical adulation. Television, films beckoned. Suddenly I knew my moment had arrived. Freddy was the turning point. Whether I used her or not, her presence allowed me a stability. Pathetic and sad, possibly, but if no one else knew the truth and if I was able to function with an imaginary partner...

If, if, if. If I could keep awake, that was more to the point. Prematurely I set myself to imagine my audience. Ideally, an audience of cat lovers; surely I could stretch my material to include dogs and budgerigars, but cat owners I was really confident in. A slow, almost apologetic start, a little uneasy shuffling, then quiet, followed by the first appreciative smiles, knowledgeable head-nodding and finally laughter. Exchanged anecdotes, instant friendships, photographs produced from inside pockets and purses, in the interval; small tufts of tail fur, a solitary white whisker in a gold or silver locket. Misty smiles, "She understood my every word." "Always up at the window, six o'clock sharp, recognised my first and neutral gears." "Timmy, Jasper, Annie, Byron, Moppett..." but could I fill a hall? How could it be advertised? Would anyone want to admit to their feline passions?

"How would you like to be a star, Edith?" Edith circled the duvet, located the hot-water bottle and settled down, easing my bedsocked feet away from the heat. She began to wash, purring happily.

I wrote, "Of course when Edith is not appearing in cabaret, she likes nothing better than monopolising the hot-water bottle."

"If mum was here, you wouldn't get any further than the bottom stair."

Below, in the hall, the telephone rang. I padded out on to the landing and leant over the banisters. I heard the answer-phone switch on, the tone, then "Hi, it's Penny. Sorry we didn't get a chance to chat yesterday. Can you and Freda come to dinner on the twenty-ninth? A small party, eight maybe ten women. Love from Jen. Byee."

***

I decided to go ahead with Freddy, but only as an imaginary lover who I'd get rid of as soon as I felt confident enough to do so. I decided to kill Freddy off immediately with the excuse that my new comedy project allowed me no time for far-flung liasons. I decided to hang on to to Freddy for as long as feasibly possible and also use her as part of my comedy routine. Surely there was a lot of mileage to be had out of Freddy and her situation, combined with the pet element. Freddy would like dogs; collies and Alsatians, nothing little or fussy. Perhaps two cats; independent animals with a sense of humour – Abyssinians. I would look up Abyssinians in the library, also spelling of same, I wrote in my notebook.

I began to write down my Freddy biography. There'd be a nucleus of friends on the South Coast, out of the way restaurants and pubs, a sporadic life of intimacy and shared concern over parents, wildlife and mutual pets. She would be constantly kept out of London. Arrangements would be made and then 'pa' would have a mini-stroke – a false alarm, but one can't be too careful – or 'Hercules', part-pointer, part-elk hound, would develop… I dismissed rabies, scabies and hardpad. More library research needed. If at any point my two worlds seemed in danger of collision, Freddy the lover could be dispensed with. I could still use her in my future act.

"Marvellous affair while it lasted. Parental pressure, the garden centre. Me never being on hand at the right time. I blame myself. It must have been dispiriting for Freddy, coming home to an empty bungalow every evening. At least Dawn's on the spot."

Yes, I'd even lined up a 'Dawn' as my successor. For me there would be imaginary tears, wiped away hastily, as I moved from friends' kitchen table to sink where I would fret unhappily at their dishcloth.

"And yet Freddy loved my work. The first woman to really be there for me. 'Gentle humour, Joan, yours is a gentle humour,' that's what she always said."

However, if 'cruel humour' turned out to be what was wanted by my audience, I would be the survivor of an emotional shipwreck; my stage act, half therapy, half incisive, bitter humour. I considered Edith for several seconds through heavy world-weary eyelids and let a cynical smile gleam in the right-hand corner of my mouth. Perhaps I should start smoking. I heard mum's voice, sharp and derisive, "Perhaps you should think about tarting yourself up a bit."

Tomorrow or the next day I would heat up my bedroom and the bathroom and take a long, warm look at what I had to offer. I was ready to change; I'd changed before, tried to be what other women had wanted. Now I would be glamorous; big and glamorous. I'd be the woman that Freddy hungered for late at night in Littlehampton.

EIGHT
Anyone who had a heart

I matched their two sofas. Had I known already that they were dove grey with navy splashes, my choice of clothes couldn't have been more successful. I leant back into the cushions; did I blend in attractively or disappear altogether? Either could be a positive. I almost regretted the thin zigzag of fuchsia running through the material of my new dress.

I hadn't worn a dress in years and never one like this: posh shop bought, grown-up, blue and grey silk. I rustled each time I crossed my legs, which I did often in an attempt to see my calves and shoes in profile. I was particularly anxious over my shoes. They had a fat heel and an ankle strap, smoky grey suede, leather soles. They made me uneasy. My feet felt swollen above and below the ankle strap and then again, the leather and suede – Penny and Jenny were vegetarians.

"You're not asking them to eat your shoes," muttered a voice behind my throbbing left eye. I'd bought a new bra as well. I had been astonished at the impressive cleavage I possessed once my breasts were gathered up and settled side by side. I felt like Elizabeth Taylor in *Cleopatra*, only Elizabeth Taylor *now*. No, I felt like Joanie Littler with Elizabeth Taylor's breasts, but not her looks, and there wasn't a centimetre of space available for any importune asp either.

"Freddy's mother needs constant surveillance," I said to Deirdre, a woman I'd never met before. Immediately I regretted 'surveillance', it made Freddy sound like a prison warden. However, Deirdre was leaning forward looking sympathetic.

"Parents are such a worry."

"Freddy does what she can, but she has her job. She's a horticulturist."

"How rewarding. Sash, Joanie's partner is a horticulturist! You two will have to get together to discuss your alpine garden."

Sash, a tall woman with lilac hair, a patchwork shirt and a headband, approached us with a freshly opened wine bottle.

"I'm afraid it hasn't had time to breathe."

Deirdre and I both shrugged sympathetically and held out our glasses.

"Have you known Jenny and Penny long?" Sash asked, sitting on the arm of the sofa.

"Penny, yes. Since before she went to college."

"Really?" they both said together, as if I'd just imparted a most startling and original fact. I found their reaction encouraging.

"Yes, we go way back. It's the first time I've been in the

house before, although of course I've been in the garden. The 'Epiphany' party," I said.

"We missed that. We always try to get away somewhere warm in January. Crete this year. It's so restful out of season, isn't it Sash?"

"A bit too restful," Sash levered herself off the arm and studied a large Diane Arbus print that monopolised one wall.

"That's very nice," said Deirdre.

"Is it?" Sash's mood seemed to have taken a turn for the worse; she read out morosely, "A woman with her baby monkey 1971."

It reminded me of myself and Edith. The monkey, a tiny animal, was dressed in baby clothes. It lay in the lap of an attractive woman in a one-piece trouser suit.

"I always imagine dressing Edith in baby clothes – just for a laugh. She won't sit still long enough, that's the trouble."

That startled them. They both stared at me, eyes wide, lips slightly parted.

"She's my cat. You know how one gets with pets."

It seemed they began to breathe again. They laughed with relief and, I thought, a little disappointment.

"We're just as mad about Toby. He's a terrier. Sash carries him up to bed at night. He has to be carried, otherwise he just sits at the bottom of the stairs and howls. Doesn't he, Sash?"

Sash's good humour was restored; she smirked unwillingly into her wine glass, "Yes, he's a silly sod but we love him."

"Edith's unreliable – never the same mood two days in a row. Steff says she takes after me."

"Steff?"

"Not 'Steff', Deirdre. Sorry, wrong girlfriend. Freddy. Freddy says she takes after me."

"So Freddy does get up to London now and then?"

"Oh yes. Well not any more. In the old days – early days – but no, not any more. Her parents, as I said, they can't be left – he's tricky, and she's, you know," I tapped my head, "and I can't take Edith down there because of Bertie the budgie. He'd make one mouthful for Edith. Freddy would be heartbroken. They're very close."

Jenny came in from the kitchen waving an open bottle of white wine. When she saw the opposing red, she frowned. "I chilled this especially."

A hatch painted to look like a small bookcase, which I hadn't noticed before, was pushed open, and Penny's flushed face appeared in front of a steam-filled rectangle. "Jenny, I told you, Sash and Deirdre only drink red."

"But I thought Joan might like this. It's Portuguese. They've really come on as a wine-producing country."

I gulped down my remaining inch of red wine and held out my glass, hoping Sash and Deirdre wouldn't think I was a) over eager, b) an alcoholic, or c) greedy, the type of woman desperate to say 'Yes' to anything that was on offer.

"They've always produced good wine," Penny said, deserting the hatch for kitchen doorway, "I'm sure Joan's had Portuguese wine before."

"Well, actually… no. It is delicious." I licked my lips enthusiastically. Somehow I'd consumed half the glass in the first sip. Penny placed a wooden hand-turned bowl of peanuts on the woven rug between the two sofas.

"There are dips on the desk," she pointed with a wet ladle, "You're not looking after our guests, Jenny. I can't do the cooking and be in here as well."

Jenny, ignoring her, continued, "But the quality has improved hundreds of percents, whatever you say."

She filled a glass taken from one of the place settings on the table and drank with her eyes closed.

"For God's sake, Jen, don't overdo things this evening," Penny hissed tightly on her way back towards the kitchen. Sash and Deirdre crunched loudly and nervously on peanuts while I headed across the room to investigate the dip situation.

"Guacamole, Joan," Jenny said, leaning on my shoulder, "I make it myself. I'm known for my guacamole in Islington."

It was lime green and runny and wouldn't balance on my celery stick, but Jenny was already off, back towards the bottle of Portuguese. "Lovely," I shouted after her. "Delicious," I nodded appreciatively in Deirdre's and Sash's direction.

"Does Bertie say much?" Deirdre asked as I returned to the settee, munching with a certain sophistication on a piece of carrot.

"Pardon?"

"Does Bertie say much?"

I repeated the question silently. Who was Bertie? Did she mean Freddy? Surely I wouldn't have mentioned a girlfriend called Bertie? Short for 'Alberta' perhaps?

"The budgie," Sash grinned at me.

"Oh, the budgie. Sorry. I better slow down," I pointed to my empty glass, "I don't drink much with Freddy. Mineral water ad infinitum, and a glass before and a glass after is her maxim."

"Before and after what?"

"Sash, that's not very nice," Deirdre looked embarrassed.

"Dinner, of course," I smiled broadly. That's how my smile felt: a good, broad, woman of the world smile; only it was hard to recall my lips back into their usual shape afterwards and my head felt top-heavy.

"Yes, Bertie does talk. Never stops actually. Chatters away to himself in his mirror. Nothing very original. 'Pretty boy, who's a pretty boy, Bertie's a pretty boy.' "

At that moment the doorbell and telephone both rang. Jenny jumped up from her distant chair by the door, and ran out of the room carolling, "Coming everybody," in a welcoming, cheery voice none of us had heard so far that evening.

I said insincerely, "I feel a little nervous without Freddy on hand – not knowing anyone."

Actually I felt buoyant. I knew that feeling. It was a danger sign. It meant that already, with the meal not even begun, I'd drunk too much.

"Don't be nervous," said Sash. Deirdre, encouraging, shook the almost empty bowl of peanuts at me: "You know us now."

"Hardly." I tried out a small pathetic laugh.

"Nonsense," said Deirdre, "You have a cat, Freddy's got Bertie, and we have our Toby. Pet owners always have their love of animals as a common bond."

I thought almost tearfully what a thoroughly pleasant, well-meaning woman Deirdre was. I said, "You're very lucky, Sash," but both their heads were turned expectantly towards the open door.

"Just leave your coats in the bedroom at the top of the stairs," Jenny was saying, voice still cheerful. "Who was that on the phone, Pen?"

"Debbie and Carol can't come. Carol's been in a darkened room all afternoon with one of her heads."

"I do not believe it," Jenny followed her resumed annoyed voice in from the hall. "I do not –" she began to manhandle two chairs away from the table "– believe it."

"I'll do that." Penny tried to pull a chair from her and we silently watched them scuffling. "Leave it, Jenny, for god's sake, top up Joan's wine."

Jenny left it and said bitterly to no one in particular, "Lesbians are notoriously unreliable."

"Oh, I don't know," I murmured, "straight couples can be pretty temperamental." And added, "Freddy's mother has terrible migraines."

No one paid the slightest attention to this opening medical gambit. Suddenly Jenny was smiling. A lovely charming smile that bypassed all of us and flew straight to the tall, middle-aged woman standing in the doorway. I saw a tanned blur of face and dazzling white, ridiculously ruffled shirt.

"Susan, what a fabulous shirt. You look great."

And there she was – my Susan. In the centre of Jenny and Penny's tasteful living room. I remembered, years ago, Susan telling me of Paddy and Clare's flat, a flat of 'muted colours', and I thought that anywhere Susan was, would always be a place of muted colours, because she was so very vibrant and alive. Behind her stood a small slim woman; hardly a woman, at most in her early twenties. Cheekbones, hip bones, blonde straight hair hanging each side of her pretty face like the ends of a long fringed scarf, reaching down to skim her neat tanned navel.

"Friends," said Susan, "this is Angela, but I call her Angel Baby."

I blinked the stars from my eyes and held out my hand. I said briskly, "Susan and I are old friends," in an easy, comfortable voice.

"Joanie, I didn't recognise you."

She moved confidently towards me, her lips were cool and dry on my hot cheek.

"It's Joan now, only Freddy calls me 'Joanie' these days." I managed a brief efficient smile, turned to the woman with her, "And what do we call you? Angel Baby or is it just plain Angela?"

"Never plain, but call her Angel," Susan said with a smile. I decided to avoid using her name completely.

***

Initially Angel had little to say for herself, for which I mentally awarded her a black mark. The result would have been the same had she been the most articulate woman at the table.

Penny had positioned her opposite me, with Susan at the end, between us. I had my back to a large gold-framed mirror. Angel Baby (in my head I used her full name derisively), spent the first course (crème vichyssoise garnished with grated carrot – not the most appropriate soup for a snowy evening), looking past me entirely and admiring her own entrancing reflection. Obviously bored by our conversation of 'where we were at' in the Sixties and early Seventies, she patted and checked out her perfect chin, tracing her jawline with the oval pearly nail of her index finger as if to emphasise the difference between her complete lack of excess flesh and our abundance. Or my abundance. I had an overwhelming desire to count my own chins. Were there two or three these days? How awful to have so many chins that I was no longer sure of the precise amount. As my fingers strayed to my jawline, Angel Baby dipped a point of her creamy-coloured hair into the soup and, after swishing it back and forth a couple of times, drooped it across the rim of her plate and then sucked it suggestively, her eyes slanting towards Susan.

I was reassured at least by Jenny, who was watching Angel Baby as narrowly as I was, twirling the stem of her wine glass as if trying to bore a hole in the tablecloth. Susan was oblivious. She was talking across me to Sash and

Penny who both had full soup spoons balanced inches from their mouths.

"I've always had Fords. They're the most reliable of the lot. I know, I know, they had a reputation for overheating – old news, not any more. That was in the bad old days," she said, as if in response to the whole table having taken up cudgels against Ford engines.

"So when were the bad old days?" I asked with a tight smile.

"Before your time, Joan. Angel, don't suck your hair at the table, there's a good girl."

"This soup's delicious, Susie. I like cold soup. It's so extraordinary. You must get the recipe."

Susan patted her hand and said to us all in the novel, transatlantic accent she was using, "I don't need the recipe. I've more cook books than I know what to do with. Anyway, I rarely get a chance to cook these days."

"She's too busy looking after me," Angel Baby pouted prettily.

"Just eat."

"Awight."

Deirdre broke bread and leant towards me encouragingly, "You and Freddy must come over one evening, or an afternoon, if that's any easier. Or come on your own. You'd be very welcome. You're a gardener as well, aren't you?"

"Not trained. I'm more maintenance. It's difficult – Freddy comes up so rarely. We have so little time together."

"What car does Freddy drive?" Susan asked.

"Nothing very impressive. A small, red van. I wouldn't know the make."

"She's never thought of getting a Ford Escort van?"

"Not to my knowledge," I replied severely, as if Susan was in danger of making a social gaffe. My glass was empty again. The wine, my bosoms resting resentfully behind my plate, were taking me over. I stared with blatant disapproval at the silver buckle of Susan's snakeskin belt. It was shaped like the head of a cobra, its eyes winked redly. "Fake rubies," I muttered under my breath.

Jenny, who I was dimly aware of as a kindred angry presence at the other end of the table, suddenly leapt to her feet and started gathering up plates.

"Hold on to your bread knives everybody," she said loudly, clattering plates down towards me.

"Jen, we've plenty of knives, as you well know," Penny remonstrated. She was still wearing her yellow plastic apron with the words 'Head Cook' in capitals on the bib, 'and Bottlewasher' in smaller italics across the skirt. Jenny smiled ruefully at Susan in particular and said with brittle gaiety, "Penny doesn't have to stack the dishwasher at one in the morning."

Angel Baby ran her small pink tongue up the blade of her knife and then attempted to lick the tip of her dainty nose. I wondered how she could breathe with such small nostrils. I looked resentfully at Susan, who was wiping up the last of her soup with a chunk of French bread.

I said lightly, "So how long did you stay in America, Susan? I only ask because the transatlantic drawl sits rather uneasily on nasal Brummie," which didn't sound light at all.

Everyone was stopped in their social tracks. Even Angel Baby paused between nose and tongue exercises and swivelled her eyes towards mine for the first time that evening. Only Jenny remained untouched by my sudden hostility, rattling plates and cutlery as if her life depended on it. Susan's easy smile stayed in place, but I sensed a tiny defensive note creep into her voice.

"It's never bothered me, having a Brummie accent. I'm not trying to hide it. Obviously, travelling around America for five years, I couldn't help but pick up different speech patterns."

"Oh-ho, speech patterns?" I queried.

"Well Joan, there's not a hint of the Midlands left in your voice. You look and sound middle-class London, and very nice too. Actually, I have been told my accent was rather sexy," she twinkled at us all.

"Good gracious," I said with a small, well-bred laugh, "I am surprised. Who thinks Susan's accent is sexy?"

"I do," Jenny called on her way to the kitchen.

"So do I," said Angel Baby.

"And how old are you?" I asked sweetly.

"Why?"

"I just wondered. You seem quite young."

"For what?"

"Well for Susan."

"I like *some* older women. They make me feel secure. No, that's not true. I don't like older women, I just like

Susan." She began to saw at the edge of the table with her knife, her lower lip trembled, "I love Susan."

I looked across at Deirdre and Sash. They were smiling and nodding kindly at her, as if to an unhappy child. Susan smiled tenderly at her and said, "Angel Baby loves me and I love her as a daughter. I've known her since she was a tot. Caroline, her mother, is a woman I used to care very much about." Her gaze flickered to me and I remembered a beautiful woman in a scarlet evening dress. "Didn't work out. End of story. Angel's staying with me for a few days before she joins her mum in Spain. All clear everyone? You too, Joan, before you reduce us all to tears?"

"That's not very fair," I said, "Obviously I was curious. Nothing wrong in being curious."

"We were all curious, weren't we, Sash?"

Sash nodded agreeably at Deirdre. They both nodded at Susan. "I'm sure Joan didn't mean to upset anyone. It's not easy for her without Freddy."

"I better help Jenny," Penny said, pushing back her chair.

"I'll come with you, we need some more wine." Susan stood up and for some reason squeezed my shoulder. Seconds later the kitchen erupted into noisy, good-natured life.

"Jen, Pen. Where is it for god's sake, we're all dying of thirst out there."

"Susan, please. This kitchen's not big enough for three."

"It's plenty big enough for three."

I looked across at Angel Baby. Her young face was pale and sad. She was still fiddling with her knife. I said, "I'm very sorry, it's the demon drink; it brings out the wicked witch in me."

"Susan is a smashing person," she said quietly, "when you get to know her."

"I'm sure she is." That was the best I could do. I felt sour with myself, with the whole evening.

Jenny and Susan came in from the kitchen, both laughing, bearing steaming serving dishes above their heads. Penny flustered, face flushed and sweating, followed them with a salad bowl and a bottle of wine: "Please be careful you two, that's the last of the Spode."

NINE
1994
Joan Littler puts pen to paper

It was my birthday last week. Freddy bought me a two-pound box of Belgian chocolates and a black satin camisole. We shared a vegetable lasagne in the Bonsai Garden in Worthing town centre. It used to be a Chinese take-away, but no interest from the locals. Then they tried Mexican to attract a younger element, only there isn't a younger element in Worthing. Well, there's the very young, but they're still at school and only have pocket money. Anyway, now the restaurant's Italian and there's talk of painting out 'Bonsai' and squeezing in something more general in case of future changes.

I lowered my fork of lasagne and looked at Freddy. She was wearing a white frilly shirt and the embroidered waistcoat I'd bought her from The Tibetan Shop at Christmas. I said, "Freddy darling, this weekend, as it is my birthday week, let's do something really special."

She smiled, her eyes changed to the greeny blue of a turbulent sea. She took the fork from my hand and chewed my lasagne thoughtfully. "I think they put more pepper on yours than on mine," she whispered.

"My birthday," I reminded her prettily.

"*Darling, of course we'll do something special. Don't we always?*"

"*Last year we went to a jumble sale. I'd really like to have a happy, social day spent with other women.*"

"*You mean, I'm not enough?*"

"*You know I don't mean that.*"

"*Do I?*" she smiled quizzically, "*It was a Guide jumble sale, not just any old jumble sale, I could have picked Sea Scouts, Ramblers, or Friends of the Earth. There was that lovely woman in the navy beret who gave you a cup of tea and two free biscuits.*"

"*I thought we could do something in London for a change.*"

"*You won't get two free biscuits in London, Joanie.*"

I tried again.

We were watching television at her house. Freddy had brought in fish and chips and we cuddled up on her tartan settee which she bought with me in mind, because tartan, particularly Black Watch, has certain sentimental associations in my life.

I was trying to tempt her away from the television, dipping my chips in tomato sauce and holding them a couple of inches from her mouth so she had to snap at them. I love the way her teeth close on a chip; it's very stimulating, all the muscles of her neck tense.

After half a dozen chips she wouldn't do it any more, became a little tetchy, said, "Go easy Joan, I want to see what the weather girl's got to say for herself, it should have been twenty-seven degrees today."

I nuzzled her ear and said, "I bet you're wondering what she's wearing under that tight red suit?"

She said, *"Funny you should mention red, I was wondering how many pounds of Moneymaker tomatoes I'd have off the allotment this year."*

"Fibber," I whispered and began to play with her earlobe, *"Let's be sinful."*

She said, *"Where?"*

I said, *"Here, in front of the fire."*

She said, *"With the budgie?"*

I said, *"No, with me, silly."*

She said, *"I don't like him watching."*

I said, *"He's not watching, he's looking in his mirror."*

She said, *"He's watching us over his shoulder."*

I said, *"Budgies don't have shoulders. Put a cloth over his cage."*

She said, *"He doesn't fall asleep till after the nine o'clock news."*

"Tell him he's having an early night then, because it's his big day tomorrow."

"What's happening tomorrow?"

"I'm taking him home to play with Edith."

I tried again.

Freddy hates me living in London. She'd like me to move down to Sussex, even a flat in Brighton would be more accessible. Each time I see her, it's always the same question.

"But what do you do every evening on your own in London?"

"I sit at home with Edith Piaf and write you love letters."

"I never get any."

"That's Edith's fault; she has trouble with long words. She's working on 'humungeous' at the moment."

I checked my dictionary. No such word. I pushed the notepad to one side and put out the light. I put the light back on, crossed out 'white frilly shirt' and wrote in 'blue denim shirt'. I put out the light again.

In the dark I could see Susan as I left Jenny and Penny's. There she was scraping snow from her car windscreen. Angel Baby was just a black shadow in the passenger seat. The frill from Susan's shirt showed up as white as the snow, in the opening of her sheepskin car coat.

"Nice seeing you, Joanie," she'd called out, waving her plastic scraper at me.

I hadn't replied. I'd climbed into the back of Sash's and Deirdre's car and they'd driven me home in silence. We were all tired. I noticed Deirdre cover Sash's hand with her own as she changed up into fourth gear. They were happily tired. That was my assumption. I was so bone-weary I didn't fall asleep until nearly five o'clock the following morning.

TEN
1995
Sunshine came softly

It's the lot of big women in shabby raincoats and hand-knitted hats to pass through crowds, our presence noted yet unrecognised. Of course, Mrs Botolph would disagree: "There's no need to make a guy of yourself, Joan. You could try dressing normally. You could wear a colour for a change."

Particularly on buses with their dark interiors, I disappear, unless arguing with the conductor or my fellow travellers. It was a midweek morning and I was off to Mrs Perriman's in Camden to get her bedding plants in before it rained. She'd telephoned at eight a.m. to say the forecast was ideal. "Sunny morning giving way to showers in the afternoon. Ideal planting weather, Joan."

En route to Mrs Perriman's, the bus was tootling gently along the Essex Road, and as predicted, the sunny morning clouds were already beginning to look threatening. I wondered whether it would be quicker to get off the bus and start running or get off the bus and go home, as we were only just approaching the minor traffic hold-up around Camden Passage Antique Market. Normally I like to look at the market; the dealers dress as I dress, because even in summer it's chilly work standing around all day.

Suddenly, in the middle of my musing 'to do or not to do', a Land Rover pulled in between the bus and the pavement. Instead of staring out at pinched grey faces, I was looking up at Susan's tanned and smiling profile. She was hitting her hand on the steering wheel in time to Patsy Cline's 'Crazy'. Through her half-open window I could hear her singing how crazy and lonesome she was, with a big smile on her face for such a sad song. I looked quickly away. It would be just my luck if my raincoat of invisibility stopped working and she spotted me. Of course she didn't. Someone like Susan isn't looking out of her car window in the hope of glimpsing a slice of real life as it happens on a 73 Routemaster. Susan wouldn't be sentimentally thinking, "Isn't that Joanie's bus? I can never look at a 73 bus without a twinge of regret."

I reluctantly concentrated on the couple sitting in front of me, who were entwined in a passionate embrace. He was like a huge, hungry python. He was like two huge, hungry pythons, intent on strangling his girlfriend with both his arms and legs. He overlapped their seat; one bent, booted leg writhing out into the gangway. His leather elbow was only inches from my nose as he turned her head this way and that, slapping noisy kisses on her neck, cheeks and mouth.

These were the worst. The mouth-to-mouth kisses. Before I'd been distracted by the market and Susan, I'd already written in my notebook, "Suction, jellyfish, two rolls of wet, red rubber," and "How can she bear it?" and "Why doesn't she scream for help?"

He groaned and paused to take off his jacket, which he laid across his lap. I wrote, "He laid his leather jacket significantly across his lap." I was now staring at his pale, almost hairless arm; his knobbly elbow winked at me over the back of the seat.

"Young love," an elderly woman sitting across the aisle mouthed at me and smiled in a kindly fashion.

I leant across my seat and whispered, "Your bags are about to fall on the floor."

"Pardon?" she said and leaned forward to hear me, the movement of her body unbalancing one of her bags. It tipped into the gangway and several oranges rolled out. I left her scrabbling for them and turned my attention back to the window. Susan and the Land Rover were still outside. She was talking to someone sitting next to her who was out of sight. Dusty Springfield was in the middle of 'In the Middle of Nowhere' and I noted waspishly that Susan's musical taste hadn't matured much in twenty years – which sent me off on the tangent of twenty years ago and the meaning of 'young love'. I wrote down "Joan's definition of young love", and underlined it. Then listed "holding hands and walking in spring sunshine", which wasn't much of a list.

The traffic started to move, then the bus started to move. Susan and the Land Rover stayed put although I could hear the blare of indignant horns coming from the line of cars behind her. Surely she hadn't stalled. I couldn't imagine Susan in a car that stalled. I couldn't imagine Susan even having a puncture or an oil change.

I turned in my seat and squinted back. She was kissing her passenger. Broad daylight, ten-thirty in the morning, half of North London still loitering over coffee and croissants, and Susan was kissing her passenger. She came up for air. I could see her smile. She waved her hand out of the window to the drivers behind, then the jeep began to move. She passed my bus, turned into St John's Street. We went right towards King's Cross. The couple in front of me started to giggle although as far as I could gather not a single word had passed between them. I rummaged under my seat for my bag containing my plastic lunch box, bottled water, hand trowel and gardening gloves. I began to edge out of the seat.

I couldn't resist it. My bag was in one hand, my biro in the other, and his bare arm was still jerking up and down along the metal bar at the top of the seat as he played with her black bra strap. I stabbed my biro hard into the soft flesh of his upper arm. Such a rewarding split second. His head shot up from his prey, saliva dripping from his lower lip.

"Ow, what the...?" he cried out.

"I am so sorry. This new biro has a mind of its own." I smiled cheerfully down at him: a mad, wide-eyed smile that made my eyebrows disappear under the ribbed edge of my hat.

"She did it on purpose," I heard him saying, but by then I was jumping off the bus.

I walked briskly past King's Cross Station, down Marchmont Street and into Tavistock Square. Bugger Mrs Perriman's summer bedders.

It wasn't easy to find an unoccupied bench in what was left of the sun. More lovers. Even the alkies seemed unnaturally fond of each other that morning. And the pigeons. At the best of times I can't bear pigeons. 'Live and let live' is all very well, but that morning I was sorely tried. One pigeon in particular, or it may have been several pigeons in particular, it's hard to tell with pigeons. They hop behind a bush and who knows if it's the same pigeon hopping out on the other side? Whatever, I'll just say he or they were very pleased with themselves and I found myself muttering, "In the privacy of their own homes," which wasn't helpful.

The sun signified its approval of my desertion from duty by deciding to make a full-scale appearance. I began to mentally cool down beneath its gentle warmth. I tried to analyse my hostile feelings towards the man on the bus. Was I a man-hater? Surely not. I hadn't known many men, certainly not in any biblical sense, and also being a poor fatherless orphan, but Nurse Duggan's Geoff had always been very pleasant and even Raymond, Mrs Botolph's ex-grandson-in-law had turned out all right in a taciturn sort of way. He had waived both mine and mum's library fines on numerous occasions, not to mention all the books he'd stolen on mum's behalf when he'd become disillusioned about his prospects at the library.

I loosened my coat, took off my woollen hat and laid it next to me on the bench. The sun was so pleasant that I settled myself down in anticipation of a little snooze. My problem was I'd just seen too many happy couples and it was spring again, and there was Susan turning up after all these years. And Susan kissing Jenny, oh yes, I'd recognise fussy, ill-natured Jenny anywhere. Surely she had more than enough to be grateful for with her Islington house, Portuguese wine and pleasant, long-suffering partner. Penny began to assume sainthood in my imagination. I was livid on her behalf. I had a good mind to blow the whistle on the whole sordid affair. I settled my bottom more comfortably on the bench and mused over blackmailing Susan.

"I'd rather you didn't say anything, Joanie love, too many people are involved. If it's money you need, I can let you have five hundred quid on account, only I thought you and I meant more to each other than just filthy lucre." Susan flicking my hair away from my still pretty face.

"Pity you didn't consider that when you started your sad little affair." I would shrug away her hand and pour myself a whisky from a handy decanter.

"Joan, it's only a game. It means nothing. You've always been the one. I've been waiting for you to grow up and now you have." Follows me over to the sideboard (what sideboard? Mrs Botolph is the only person I know who owns a sideboard) and grips me roughly by the shoulders.

I look mistily into whisky glass. "You're too late Susan, twenty years too late," I murmur softly, regretfully, ruefully.

In real life, on the bench in Tavistock Square, I began to chuckle, my anger gone.

I still felt a little sad, with the pain that was an old friend, but it no longer had the power to interfere with my general good humour.

I thought about my first comedy booking – it might be a success. Nothing ventured. Life wasn't so bad, was it? I should do Mrs Perriman's garden. She was a pleasant woman. Even her two cats were pleasant, using the neighbouring gardens as their toilets, a courtesy quite overlooked by Edith. And she (Mrs Perriman) always offered me a choice of tea or coffee, plain or fruit cake. I was beginning to feel hungry. I opened my eyes and reached for my hat. In it was a pound coin and two twenty pence pieces. Could I cautiously assume that my luck was beginning to get better?

ELEVEN
Starting at the bottom

"So you see," explained Janice, who was compere and top of the bill as well as organiser, "it's in your interests as a beginner to go on first."

"Oh I quite understand, but..." Suddenly, going on at all seemed a bad idea.

"It will give you a chance to develop your act without the intimidation of a larger audience – only a sprinkling turn up for the start."

"Great, but..." My smiling lips stuck to my gums.

"We all have to start at the bottom."

"Of course, I wasn't suggesting... I just thought..."

"That's OK, then?"

I nodded. It was impossible to imagine the fair Janice starting at the bottom. Her short orange hair, matching tights and purple suede bootees, combined with a glowing self-confidence, would automatically assume star billing.

"What do you do?" I asked humbly.

"Oh god, what don't I do?" She swung a small purple foot across the dusty floor. "I'm a singer-songwriter, quite apart from holding everything together in here, which includes PR and booking, and finding fresh acts. But actually, vis à vis singing and songwriting, I'm semi-professional."

This last information was said in a clipped, business-like tone and prompted her to slide from her stool and begin a serious study of her clipboard.

"I'll introduce you about eight-thirty. Todd will have the mike up and running in ten minutes, if you want to get in an early sound check."

"I don't think I'll need a mike."

She looked dubious. "Well it's up to you. It can be noisy, even at first."

"Is there anywhere I can change?"

"There's the women's toilet, but it means you'll have to walk through the pub proper. Nothing too revealing, is it?"

"On the contrary," I smirked and patted my bulging carrier bag. A new blue hot-water bottle peaked demurely out above my tartan wool dressing gown.

"Mmmm," she replied.

I'd heard about the venue from Susan. I hadn't actually seen Susan since spotting her canoodling with Jenny in the Land Rover, but everywhere I went – and I was going out much more since my fictitious liaison with Freddy had become common knowledge – there were stories about what Susan was or wasn't doing. Somehow within a very few months she'd assumed icon status and some of her glory was rubbing off on me. I was continually being asked, just what was she really like? Had she always been that wonderful?

Intelligent women were being silly about her. Nobody wanted to know if I had been that wonderful; but on the strength of our early relationship I had been invited to parties, dinners and even two afternoon barbecues. I was a woman who by some strange, not immediately obvious to the naked eye, attraction had snared in her time at least two highly prized females – admittedly, one fictional, but there were moments when I almost believed my own publicity.

Back on Susan and this venue. A couple of weeks earlier she'd sent me a flyer:

Monthly 'women-only' performances
If you've a song to sing, or a story to tell,
pick up the phone, give Janice a bell.

On the back, Susan had scrawled, "Of any interest? Jenny tells me you've embraced 'song and dance' in a big way. Best of luck, Susan."

I had fumed for several minutes over the 'song and dance'. Why did people never listen to me? Was I so boring? Even in spite of my newly found popularity, I'd noticed people still switched off as soon as I started talking about myself or what I was doing.

"Am I so boring?" I'd asked mum, who was pretending to be asleep. This was on a sunny afternoon in the garden at Shepherd's Fennel.

"Mum, wake up. There's a ladybird on the rim of your cup."

"Que sera," she muttered, "I'm dreaming."

"And I'm trying to have a conversation with you. What do you think? Am I boring?"

She opened one eye, reluctantly the other. "You do go off the point, and your voice can get monotonous."

"Thanks very much."

"You asked."

"You've never been a supportive mother."

"You never went without jam on your bread," she snapped back. I didn't mind. It was preferable to her dozing. I only ever visit for an hour at a time, surely it's not too much to ask that she keeps awake?

On the point of Susan's receipt of misinformation, after a quiet hour and a half, musing on my train journey back to London, I tracked it down to the previous month when I'd bumped into Penny, the still-unaware cuckold. I had been loitering in Boots, Islington branch, considering my purchase of the hot-water bottle that was to be a mainstay of my then only tentative comedy act; pleasantly sited in an unspecified, distant future. I was also having a breather, because the morning had turned surprisingly warm and I'd come out in jumpers, vest and anorak. I don't like my face when I sweat. It becomes pink and pasty, or is it pink and like pastry? Unfortunately I couldn't take off the anorak, as I'd worn a stained jumper. Nothing unpleasant. Yellow paint that looked like breakfast eggs; a quantity, say four or five breakfast eggs, or several breakfasts worth of eggs.

Penny had come up on me unexpectedly. I had the hot-water bottle in one hand and I was fanning myself with a cellophane-wrapped rubber sheet which had no connection with anything, but had seemed just the right shape for a fan. Penny looked quizzically at my proposed purchases. I said, "The rubber sheet's for Freddy's father."

She said, "And the hot-water bottle? It's almost June, Joan. Frankly I can't even stand the leccy blanket in mid-winter, never mind a hotty. Jen's feet are like two flaming coals."

I could have replied, "If I had the benefit of Jen's flaming feet in my bed, I wouldn't be standing here talking to you, madam," or "You're not the only woman reaping the benefit of Jen's flaming feet." Instead I muttered, "It's a prop. I'm hoping to do some comedy sketches. You know, perform in public."

Her neat little nose wrinkled in bewilderment. "You mean perform in public?" she repeated.

"Oh this is too much," I raged under my breath, "Yes, perform. Comedy clubs, performance evenings, acoustic nights."

"And the hot-water bottle, do you blow it? Does it make a musical noise?"

"It's just a prop, that's all, not a musical instrument."

Afterwards I was sure I'd been screaming, but she continued to smile encouragingly as she began to slide away from me towards a display of toothbrushes which guaranteed total oral hygiene and the removal of plaque. Plucking a lilac brush from the shelf and dropping it into her basket, she said in a distracted way, "I'll tell Jen I've seen you."

She hesitated, her hand poised over a second lime-coloured toothbrush. "We see quite a bit of Susan these days. She and Jenny are great friends."

"Really?" I said. "How nice."

"Yes, isn't it?" She smiled a rather brave smile. "Well, bye-bye."

I watched her walk away and considered her 'bye-bye'. I wasn't irritated with her any more; I was depressed and sorry for both of us. It was un-Pennylike. It said, 'I fear the worst and dread being alone. If anything is going on I'd rather not know.'

I decided I quite liked Penny – Jenny and Susan deserved... I could think of nothing suitably appropriate, so settled on 'their come-uppance' which didn't seem half bad enough. The sunny pavement beckoned. I thought, "I'll go into McDonald's toilets and turn this jumper inside out, then I can do without my anorak."

Hand on the swing door, the aroma of my rubber purchases sweating in my warm hand reminded me that I hadn't yet paid for them. I returned to the till and bought both items, just in case Penny was still lurking somewhere in or around the shop.

"Oh I'm absolute rubbish," Janice was saying to identical twins in red and black berets. She strummed her guitar thoughtfully as if already performing.

"Nonsense, Jan," said red beret admiringly, "You're so talented. Todd says you've had offers to tour but turned them down."

Janice bent her head demurely over her guitar. "*Offer*

actually, and Todd shouldn't go spreading rumours."

It was difficult to imagine Todd spreading rumours – so far that evening he'd acknowledged no one, not even Janice, his long-term partner.

"We're trying for a baby, so touring's out for the foreseeable future."

"Ah," they both said and we all stared fondly across at Todd who was wrestling with the wires of the sound system. This prompted his first and only exchange.

"Don't watch me. I hate people watching me. Leave me alone to do the job, or get someone else."

"Sorry darling," Janice called. To me she whispered, "He's very sensitive. Don't worry, we chuck him out when the performance starts."

"Doesn't he mind?" I asked.

"No, he's glad to go. He's not comfortable around women." She strummed several bars. "Nor with men either. He's very fond of the dog so I'm sure he'll make a great father."

It was a quarter to eight and the other performers were beginning to straggle in. I helped Janice and the twins set out the chairs and tables and we forced candles into the necks of bottles and lit them. Janice taped a 'NO SMOKING PLEASE' sign on the door and called out, "Everybody, can you get your bags and coats off the stage?" in a bossy, professional manner.

I was beginning to realise that my complacency about leaving my career to ferment over the next few years might be unfounded. From the ages of my fellow performers, I was already too old by at least a decade, and to succeed even at this level I would need a bank loan. I must bring myself up to date. No more corner shop carrier bags – a rucksack in leather or good quality canvas. I would also have to master a stringed instrument. At least carry a fiddle or guitar case, although a permanently bandaged hand might be necessary to ensure I was never called on to give anybody a tune.

"I'll just play a love song I wrote for Freddy, bless her. She loves the sea." Out comes the guitar. Twiddle, twiddle. Perhaps it would be effective to at least learn how to tune it. I'd observed guitarists over the years – well certainly Susan and a very popular woman friend of Nurse Duggan's – always wasted hours tuning their instruments, picking up masses of admiration just by plinking up and down the neck of the thing with their brows furrowed as if completely per-plexed by the sounds they were producing.

"I'm sorry, that's all I'm good for. This damn hand. Freddy's mother and a pan of boiling milk I'm afraid. Her sense of balance is completely shot."

Perhaps I could buy a flute or a penny whistle, have them sticking artfully out of my top pocket. But what top pocket? I didn't possess a top pocket – and there I was, back again to the problem of no suitable clothes.

Over the years I had spent months worrying about my lack of clothes: my unsuitable existing clothes, and having no money to buy and no knowledge of what to buy, had I the money. There had been brief periods of successful dress-ing when Steff or Susan had taken a hand, but personally I'd only ever tinkered with the problem. Charity shops would no longer do. Experience had taught me that anything pretty, clean or of good quality would always be a size ten. Of course I had my grey silk dinner-party dress, but that was too formal, even for some dinner parties, which was a shame as I looked my best in formal.

I followed Janice back and forth across the room, smiling cheerfully, and dutifully saying, "Looks nice, sounds nice," and "that's nice". Inside I was desperate but determined, eaten up with greed. I wanted boots, jeans, embroidered waistcoats, gypsy skirts, silk and pure cotton shirts, belts, ethnic jewellery, regular visits to the hairdresser, highlights, exercise and dance classes – and I wanted them this week, immediately, two hours ago.

I finally ran out of candles or space on the tables to put them so I concentrated on dodging about behind Janice, hoping that my proximity to her might be interpreted as a sign of our old and valued friendship, and that thought would prevent the realisation that I looked old-fashioned, drably old-fashioned. I considered moving across to Todd and sharing a few words about his no doubt lovable dog, but Todd's temper seemed unreliable. It was better to keep with Janice, who was now almost stationary, guitar at rest on a chair. She ran through the final running order. Behind her, I swayed gently, my hands loosely clasped across my stomach, apparently almost in a trancelike state – which was only superficial, as underneath I was a raging quagmire, or inside I was a raging quagmire. Then suddenly I was no longer directly behind Janice. With a neat manoeuvre of her purple bootees, she twitched around and came to rest on one side of me.

"Everybody, this is Joan Littler," she announced, as if I'd just appeared by magic and hadn't been hanging about for forty minutes, "Our comedienne for this evening."

Everybody paused, heads were turned appraisingly towards me. I wished she'd left out 'our comedienne', I'd have rather have had 'The entertaining Joan Littler' or 'Joan Littler, the teller of strange tales' than be stuck with the obligation to be amusing.

I remembered, in my televisual childhood, an elderly Scottish actor who had recounted ghost stories sitting in an armchair by an open fire, wearing a not dissimilar dressing gown to the one in my bag. No hot-water bottle though. How to bring in a hot-water bottle for a 'teller of strange tales'?

"Joan," Janice was tugging the sleeve of my raincoat, "Do you want to say anything?"

"Not at the moment," I replied. "If you don't mind I'll save my voice for later."

"Joan's a virgin," Janice said. Nobody looked in the least surprised. "So let's all wish her a lot of luck tonight."

"Thank you. Most kind. Must get changed. Now where did I put that...?" I ducked away from their muted good wishes and went in search of my carrier bag.

I wasn't technically a virgin. The previous Sunday I'd run through my material in front of mum, Mrs Botolph, a comatose Mrs Scott and two nurses on their tea break. We were in one corner of the Shepherd's Fennel Lounge, tucked in between the piano and an outside wall, so as not to disturb the other residents who were clustered around the two television sets, watching a church ceremony and videoed snooker highlights.

Mum, who had recently seemed set on a life of quiet contemplation, roused herself enough for a well-intentioned, "I'm glad to see you've a good wool dressing gown, Joan."

The two nurses laughed twice in different places, so I counted that as four laughs. Nothing from Mrs Scott but Mrs Botolph made several amused, horselike snorts, then spoilt herself by adding, "Must everything be sexual?"

I said, "Hardly sexual, Mrs Botolph, more double entendre, and there were several Edith and budgie jokes."

"Your mother and me, we don't like mucky connotations," she'd said firmly, "But I suppose they might go down well with your Hackney cronies."

I said, "Freddy darling, will you get me an eternity ring for Christmas?"

She said, "No need, pet, there's been a ring around your bath for as long as I can remember."

She said, "You don't need one, Joanie love, there's been a ring around your neck for an eternity."

I said, "Freddy, will you still love me when I'm old and fat and wearing dentures?"

She said, "I do."

She said, "'Course I will, Joan, but I might not make the trip up to London more than once every couple of months."

"Are you reading a book in there?" a peevish voice enquired from the other side of the cubicle door.

"No."

"Because I'm waiting to go in. The other toilet's blocked."

I responded gaily in case this was my first brush with the public: "Sorry. Only a minute. I'm just getting changed."

There were a few seconds of silence as the voice digested this and I struggled out of my raincoat and rummaged for my dressing gown.

"Couldn't you get changed out here?"

"I'm coming right now." I squeezed out of the door. The contents of my carrier bag seemed to have exploded, trebled to a cabin trunk's worth of possible props.

"Are you ill?" the woman asked, her face softening slightly at my dressing gown and hot-water bottle. I saw my face in the mirror behind her. I did look as if I was running a high temperature; I was scarlet and sweating, my hair beginning to snake unattractively upwards from my forehead.

"Of course not. It's my costume. I'm on in the show upstairs."

She closed the cubicle door behind her.

"Are these yours?" Several pages of jokes were pushed towards me under the door.

I scrabbled them up from the floor and stuffed them into my dressing gown pocket. Next problem, to fill or not to fill the hot-water bottle? Was it more amusing full or empty?

Was it particularly amusing? Why was I wearing a dressing gown? There had been a reason some months ago at the beginning of the year, but now I couldn't remember it.

Behind me the toilet flushed and the woman emerged looking quite friendly. She watched me in the mirror while she rinsed her hands. "Are you famous?"

"No. This is my first time."

"You're very brave."

"Mad more like." I smiled sheepishly. I was good at being sheepish. If I could spend my whole life being successfully sheepish, I would probably... and there my imagination failed me.

"Well, good luck," she said.

Left on my own, I dwelt on whether to wear my woollen hat or to be sick in the sink. At that moment Janice popped her pretty little head around the door and said, "Oh, there you are. It's nearly time. No last minute nerves?"

"Good gracious, no." Sheepish for the moment had deserted me and my hands shook as I gathered up the contents of my torn carrier bag.

I walked back through the pub, Janice and clipboard bobbing merrily at my side, 'like a dainty sprite taking a lumbering cow for a walk,' the words popped into my mind.

"Sit at the side of the stage and wait for my intro," Janice said as she marched me up the stairs.

Contrary to Janice's prediction, the room was packed, so crowded that Todd had to bring chairs up from the pub. It was as if the word had gone around, possibly Todd rumour-mongering that something dreadful was about to happen. There was even a local reporter in the audience which, Janice assured me later, they'd never had before.

For a semi-professional singer-songwriter, Janice made a very good comedienne. She told a story about her mum and dad and her childhood in Manchester that was touching as well as amusing. I feared for my laboured Freddy jokes, the budgie and Edith – would anybody be interested, never mind amused? Would the audience start yawning and shuffling and stamp en masse down to the bar? I'd brought in my own bottle of supermarket wine and a paper cup. I'd only intended to take a few dainty sips, but before Janice was halfway through her first warm-up anecdote, I was on the refill.

She finally finished with a lyrical tribute to her mother who was sitting coquettishly on a bar stool and blocking the gangway. She was introduced as Eileen who had recently achieved the grand age of sixty. On cue, we all marvelled and clapped. I privately thought sourly that a white gypsy frock with plunging neckline was most unsuitable and why was almost the whole world beginning to look younger than me? If I wasn't careful I'd soon have the edge on Mrs Scott and chère Botolph. Janice ended in a reverential silence, finally broken by a loud sob. Everyone laughed good-naturedly and reached for their own tissues. Not good-natured at all, I thought, "Well thank you, Janice, you've made me look a complete non-starter."

"And a big welcome for our comedienne, Joan Littler,"

said Janice, running and skipping daintily backwards off stage, which even in my hostile state I grudgingly admired. Not easy, smiling, carrying a guitar, a clipboard and running backwards; a final cartwheel to take her gracefully into the wings wouldn't have surprised me.

"Thank you, Janice," I called, "It's been a long time since I skipped like that," which came out of my mouth rather bitterly. I sipped more wine and tried a smile.

The upturned, relaxed and expectant faces of my audience disconcerted me – they actually thought I was going to make them laugh. Janice had said I was a comedienne and that was good enough for them. They took in my dressing gown and hot-water bottle and generously came down in my favour. Yes I was going to be a hoot, at that moment I had them in the palm of my hand. I coughed nervously and took yet another small medicinal sip of wine.

"Actually… in actual fact, I've never skipped. Skipping is for the very young or very short," I said.

Janice's mother shouted, "Speak up."

"I am speaking up."

It was the microphone. Set up with Janice and a band of performing pygmies in mind, it only reached my breast-bone. I had no idea how to raise it, and anyway my hands were full.

"Get on with it," Janice's mother again. Birthday or no birthday, I resolved to speak to her in the break. I bent my knees so that my nose almost rested on the microphone head and bawled, "Freddy's my girlfriend. Short for Freda which is short for Frederika. She looks after her invalid parents in a bungalow in Littlehampton."

I took a larger sip of wine to prevent my tongue sticking to the roof of my mouth.

"For Christmas I took her mother a box of diabetic chocolates and bought her dad a good quality shopping bag from the Argos Catalogue. We spent the whole afternoon watching a video of Pavarotti in a dress with the sound turned off." (Pause for appreciative titter – silence.) "Afterwards in the kitchen, making cocoa for four, Freddy said, "Joan, just a word. It's dad who's the diabetic, mum's angina and was there any particular reason for buying him that shopping bag?"

I said, "You said your dad's bag kept leaking with the weight of his amber liquid, so I bought him something more substantial to bring his beer home in."

"I meant 'catheter', Joan."

"Well write it down and next time I'll see if the off-licence stocks it."

I stopped again. Still absolute silence. I tried to read the general expressions on the faces at the front. They'd changed from smiling to impassive. My knees were hurting so much from bending, I was forced to straighten up which unbalanced me a little. The full hot-water bottle wobbled from my restraining arm and hit my paper cup, sending wine over the microphone. There was a small flash and a sizzling noise. My left knee – always the weak one – buckled beneath me and my head shot forward, hitting the mike hard. With a cry of anguish, I hurled the hot-water bottle into the audience and for some reason threw myself, spread-eagled, from the stage. In the split second of my falling, a hand flashed out and whipped away the bottle with the lighted candle from the table I was about to land on. All went dark, as they say, and I knew no more until the moment my stretcher entered the crowded public bar.

Someone had kindly laid my hot-water bottle across my stomach and folded my hands over it. My head rested on my carrier bag and my dressing gown was decently draped, the blanket-stitched lapels flat and firm across my breasts.

"Is she dead?" a male voice enquired.

"No, they'd have covered her face," was the sympathetic reply.

I had three badly bruised ribs and four stitches in the cut on my forehead. There was a picture on the front page of the local paper of me lying face down on a table amongst tipped paper cups, and a smaller one of Janice hugging her mother.

Susan left a message on my answerphone, Sash and Deirdre sent flowers and a photograph of their garden taken at dusk. On the back they'd written, "Get well soon. You've missed the azaleas. Love Sash, Deirdre and baby Toby (bottom right)."

I searched 'bottom right' and sure enough there was a small white smudge that could have been Toby's face or for that matter could just as well have been his bottom.

Then there was an open dinner invitation from Jenny and Penny, a letter on lilac notepaper of the 'much the sort of behaviour I'd expect from you Joan' variety from Mrs Botolph and a note from Matron at Shepherd's Fennel saying mum was smoking too much and could I not bring in any more cigarettes.

Several days later, after some 'should I, shouldn't I's', I rang Susan.

"It's Joan," I said, "Thanks for the message and the flowers."

"I didn't send flowers."

"Exactly, but never mind."

"Joanie," she sounded slightly drunk, "How are you? I did cut your picture out of the *Echo*. I'm thinking of having it enlarged. Anyway what's happening your end?"

"Nothing much is happening my end. My ribs will be painful for a few weeks, but there won't be any facial scarring."

"Good, I'm glad you're all right." She sounded quite sincere.

I took a deep breath and said, "The thing is, Susan, I'd like to borrow some money."

"There are banks," she sounded sincerely cautious.

"I'm not good with banks."

"How much?"

"Five hundred."

She whistled, "That's a lot of money. What do you want it for?"

"I want to buy clothes and have my hair done."

She was silent for a moment, then came the familiar, irregular breathing that meant she was chuckling.

"OK Joanie," she laughed now, "Cash or cheque?"

TWELVE
1996
Thank you, Mrs Scott

A humid, damp day in July; I sat on a garden wall adjacent to the bus stop imagining myself invisible, part of the bus queue while not actually in it, ready to claim my position as fifth in the line, the second a 73 bus circled the roundabout.

I wore a long, black cotton cloak with a generous hood, bought the previous week in the Dalston branch of Oxfam. Not suitable for summer, but I felt the light drizzle fully justified my wearing it. 'Enshrouded' was the word that kept popping into my head, which may have had something to do with being on the way to Mrs Scott's funeral.

I'd known Mrs Scott since I was small; we'd met on her fifty-fifth birthday when mum and I had been invited to tea. I'd been sullen about going, mum having told me to keep my mouth shut and eat what was put in front of me, which prompted one of my too clever by half remarks, followed by one of mum's frequent pocket money withdrawals.

I liked Mrs Scott immediately. With such a mother I'd have been a daintier child, and at that time I craved to be dainty, fragile and feminine; virtues that held no appeal whatsoever as far as mum was concerned.

At that first tea party, Mrs Scott served delicate meringue shells, coconut castles and tiny squares of Genoese sponge covered in pastel icing. She was the mistress of the small decorative cake. Her tea, which mum refused to drink, was weak but a beautiful ivory colour. I never saw what Mr Scott ate or drank – he kept to the front room – but mum said "She" (Mrs Scott) "didn't feed him enough to keep a mouse alive," which wasn't very loyal of mum, and in any case Mr Scott lived well into his seventies, finally being knocked down by a reversing refuse lorry and even then hanging on for a further eleven weeks.

We all had to visit him in hospital, or at least we visited the corridor outside the intensive care unit, as only Mrs Scott was allowed in. Mrs Botolph said, "That man's got the constitution of an ox," to which mum and me both nodded and puffed out our cheeks in despair because by then we were getting weary of the visiting and the constant being prepared for the worst. When Mrs Scott finally staggered out into the corridor late one afternoon (we were sitting on a long plastic banquette fingering our invalids' fruit and talking about the exorbitant price of cinema tickets), we'd almost forgotten why we were there. She whispered, "He's gone," in tragic tones; Mrs Botolph patted her gently on the shoulder and said, "Gone where, dear?"

Mum brought that day's fruit home and sent me out for double cream to have with stewed apple and apricot, all of which possibly tells you more about us than about Mrs Scott.

Returning to my cheerfully invisible day, I'd started on a crossword at the back of the gardening magazine I'd bought for mum, the rain was making a serious effort to turn into a downpour. I pulled my hood further forward over my face which cut off the view of everybody to just above their ankles. Seven pairs of summer shoes and sandals, all standing in the wet. Not me, in my solid, flat-heeled, black leather boots. Ideal for puddles and walking in muddy cemeteries. Not one of those people could have successfully attended a burial in the South East that day. I tut-tutted smugly over the world and its partner ignoring weather forecasts, and where was the point of a Meteorological Office if we all took no notice of its advice, then I returned to the crossword, clue, 'root vegetable', six letters.

Several yards away I could hear a car horn, blaring insistently. I didn't look up. Car horns were for school children or women wearing tight leggings, never for me. Number three in line; a woman in Scholl sandals whose umbrella was dripping on my cloaked knees, sidestepped in my direction, not quite enough to lose her place. She tapped the top of my hood with an umbrella spoke.

"It's you she's hooting," she said.

"Pardon?" I said.

"Her over there. Holding up the traffic. Get a move on, the bus can't get past."

It was Susan's Land Rover, lights flashing, Susan hanging out of the passenger window. I ran, I hoped gracefully, towards her.

"Joan, are you bloody deaf?" she shouted as I gathered up

the wet skirt of my cloak and climbed up and in.

"How did you recognise me?" I asked breathlessly.

"Well, you're probably the only woman in London wearing a get-up like that in the middle of the summer."

"It's raining," I mumbled.

"It's still bloody hot. Anyway, where are you off to?" She cruised over a changing amber light.

"Worthing, via Victoria Station," I said, "You'd better let me off at the next bus stop."

We drove past the next two bus stops in silence. Finally Susan said, "Your mum all right?"

"Yes, but Mrs Scott died at the weekend. I'm going down for her funeral."

"I thought she died years ago," Susan said unsympathetically. "She must be at least a hundred and ten." She'd never been fond of mum and her cronies, nor they of her.

"Mrs Scott was only eighty-six," I said.

"Only eighty-six. How old's Ma Littler, then?"

"Mum's well into her eighties. Susan, you'd better drop me off. You can't take me all the way to Victoria."

"I wasn't intending to. I fancy a day by the sea. I'll drive you down, unless you're meeting up with Fearless Freddy."

I didn't rise to the bait. For once I couldn't bring myself to lie, or not with any imagination. "No, Freddy's... busy. Thank you."

I took off my cloak and put it on the back seat with my carrier bag. Susan glanced sideways at me, "That's a nice dress, Joan. Black suits you."

"Does it?" I asked innocently, trying to spread out my

flattened hair becomingly with my fingers. It began to rain even harder, grey clouds racing tempestuously across the sky. "I bought it with your money – don't worry, I'll pay you back."

"I'm not worrying."

I tried to relax, it was only Susan sitting next to me. Pretend I'd hitched a lift from a long-distance lorry driver, nothing threatening – a home-loving man with wife, three kids and an arthritic mother living in the next road – which brought me back to thinking about my mum and Mrs Scott and Mrs Botolph.

For the past eight years, mum and Mrs Scott had shared a pretty pink and lilac painted room at Shepherd's Fennel, with Mrs Botolph visiting twice weekly. Slowly, during that time, Mrs Scott had withdrawn into herself, rarely speaking or even smiling, except on odd occasions, when the sun made a rainbow across her bedcover, or if she suddenly caught sight of mum. Mrs Botolph often mouthed 'senile' to mum over the top of Mrs Scott's white curls, which sounds cruel but I'm sure wasn't meant to be – Mrs Botolph prides herself on calling a spade a spade, but underneath she can be quite sentimental. Mrs Scott didn't really seem senile, more 'elsewhere', and as long as I'd known her, she'd often seemed 'elsewhere', even when preparing butterfly sponges or discussing the natural beauty of her aunt's rag rugs.

I was saddened by her death, but it had been expected for some time, and my sadness hadn't stopped me from becoming irritated with Mrs Botolph's high-handedness in ordering me down to Littlehampton for the day.

"For goodness sake, Joan, wear something suitable," she'd droned on over the telephone, "No nose rings or visible tattoos if you don't mind."

"I have neither, Mrs Botolph," I'd answered stiffly.

"Don't be cute, Joan, you get my drift. You'll need a decent black jacket and sensible shoes. Something for your head. Your mother will expect it."

"Mum wouldn't expect anything like that," I'd argued. I heard Mrs Botolph clicking her false teeth over my perceived stubbornness.

"Send your mother a pretty condolence card," she continued, "and organise some flowers from you both. She's very upset. We all are."

She sniffed and blew her nose which upset me more than anything. Mrs Botolph being her usual bossy self I could deal with, Mrs Botolph giving way to tears seemed awful.

"Oh come on now, she was a good age," I said.

"Only seven years older than I am, Joan, that's no age at all."

"But her health was indifferent. You're very spry, young for your years."

Comforted, she snapped back into her normal state, "Your mother and I won't live for ever. Your place is down here. You should consider moving," she said sharply.

"I do have a career, Mrs Botolph." We were back on familiar ground.

"There's plenty of gardens want digging on the coast."

"I'm talking about my professional career. As a comedienne."

I could hear my voice, not at all light and amusing. Pompous. I could have been saying, "A brain surgeon."

"Joan, I have to prepare for a funeral."

"Surely Mrs Scott's relations are dealing with it."

"There are other things," she said ominously, "Think on."

The telephone went dead.

I had no intention of 'thinking on'. I thought 'what a bloody cheek that woman had' and went in search of Edith, napping under the variegated weigela, called "Fish" and "Dinner" several times loudly into her one visible ear. Finally she obliged me by standing up and stretching both front and back legs, taking several steps across the lawn before rolling on her back and fixing me with mad, staring eyes. Reassured that, physically at least, she was in good shape, I went indoors to consider something suitable.

By the time we reached the nursing home some hours later it had stopped raining, but a cold wind now whipped around the crush of people milling around the front garden and drive. I left Susan to park farther along the road and went in search of mum.

The hearse was already there, coffin inside, flanked by several solemn men in dark coats and an elderly woman who I assumed was the daughter we'd heard about over the years but never seen. I headed towards Matron who was trying to herd a party of eight residents into a mini-bus.

"Doris, you are already wearing your coat," she bawled at

a small woman in a raincoat and headscarf, then she spotted me and smiled. "Oh hello Joan, god give me strength. I'll swing for this lot one of these days."

I liked Matron. She was one of the few people who remembered my name, and not because they'd used it on so many occasions to emphasise an unwelcome point.

"Hello Matron," I said, fielding Miss Douglas who'd started to sprint towards the open front gate. "Is everyone going to Mrs Scott's funeral?"

"Not quite. It's really an outing rather than a funeral for most of our residents. Your mum's in her room with Mrs Botolph. If you could hurry them up. Mrs Scott's going to be late for her own funeral at the rate everybody's going."

I don't know what I expected from mum – sulks, tears, a withdrawal – but no, it was Mrs Botolph who was sitting on the edge of mum's bed sniffing noisily into a tissue. Mum was standing in front of her, supporting herself on her walking stick to which she'd tied a festive red bow. She was patting Mrs Botolph's head roughly rather as if she was a large dog.

"There, there, B," she said, "Better stop now. Joan will have a field day if she finds you in tears."

"Thanks very much, mum," I said, entering the room in a flurry of damp, black cotton. "I would have no such thing."

"Joan, don't creep up on people. We could have both had heart attacks," mum squawked.

Mrs Botolph's tears had miraculously soaked away into her quarter-inch-thick layer of powder; her small mascaraed eyes blinked rapidly over me.

"You can't wear that," she said, "You look like a ghoul."

"Ghouls wear white," I said.

"Joan, you do it on purpose. You'll just have to wear something of your mother's."

She was on her feet now, balled tissue aimed accurately at the distant wastepaper basket as she headed for mum's wardrobe.

"This will do –" the wooden coat-hangers clattered angrily "– dressy but at least it shows respect for the dead."

"I don't wear fur," I remonstrated. She advanced on me with a black, beaver lamb jacket.

"Wear it, Joanie," this was Susan, leaning against the door frame, an amused expression on her face.

"Oh my gawd," shouted mum, who had recently begun to resemble an ancient parrot, "Look what the cat's dragged in."

It was nearly twenty years since either of them had clapped eyes on Susan and both were still determined to be hostile. Mum circled painfully around her, keeping a safe distance, walking stick at the ready as if expecting Susan to lunge.

"Hello Mrs Littler, Mrs Botolph," Susan gave each a neat nod of the head, "Both as gorgeous as ever."

"Huh," mum said.

"Don't try your smarmy tricks on us," Mrs Botolph snapped as she adjusted her corset through the silk of her dress. "Joan, get that jacket on."

I put it on. It smelt of mothballs and Edith drying out after a night on the tiles.

"What do you think?" I asked Susan, doubtfully.

"You look great. Like a film star. Don't worry."

"Don't anyone say anything about how *we* look," Mrs Botolph said petulantly.

"Come on, B," mum said, prodding her lightly in the buttocks with the end of her stick. "We're off to a funeral, not a garden party. Joan, help me on with my coat. I hope you ordered the flowers to my specifications."

Mum was having difficulty with the ends of her pink chiffon scarf and didn't pick up on my reluctant "Sort of".

Later, in the Land Rover, following the funeral procession at break-neck speed down the narrow Sussex lanes, Susan asked, "What were your mum's specifications?"

"Oh them. They were ridiculous. She wanted 'TO A DEAR FRIEND' in woven antirrhinums, fifteen inches high, pink and yellow mind you. It would have cost a fortune, even if I could persuade a florist to do it in the first place."

"Did you try?"

"No." I grinned, but guiltily. "It just wasn't sensible."

"It wasn't sensible, mum," I was saying later as I supported her along the gravel path outside the church. On each side, laid out on the grass, were bouquets and tributes. Mrs Scott, in her own gentle way, had been very popular. We were walking slowly as mum insisted on reading and commenting on every card.

"They particularly couldn't oblige with the antirrhinums."

"They can do anything these days," mum said sulkily. "It isn't as if microchips were involved."

Sometimes mum knows too much for my own good. We both sighed, for very different reasons, which brought us level with our nice, white chrysanthemum cross.

"The florist said white chrysanthemums were always most acceptable."

"She would, wouldn't she. Common as muck."

"Well it was that or lilies and you don't like lilies."

"They both smell of death," mum said gloomily.

"Perhaps that's why they're considered appropriate then."

"Couldn't you have ordered dahlias or red carnations? All florist shops do red carnations." Mum sounded quite desolate.

"That's not the point," I persisted, "Floral tributes are generally in pale colours. It is a pretty card."

She turned it over and read out, "To my dear friend, Mrs Scott. Love Dolly. Plus Joan."

"Yes, it is quite nice." She rummaged in her pocket for a hanky. "I don't suppose it matters," she said, "I just wanted to make a bit of a splash. So Mrs Scott would spot it and know."

I opened my mouth to say, "But Mrs Scott's dead," then shut it again. I could have howled myself, but what good would that have done? Mrs Botolph was approaching us from the other end of the lines of flowers, dabbing at her eyes with one of her gloves.

"Got a tissue, Dolly?" she asked.

As always mum had a pocket pack of Kleenex to distribute. I took two and went in search of Susan.

A late afternoon sun had come out. All the clouds were dispersing towards the horizon and the wet grass and flowers sparkled with drying raindrops. Even as a child I'd liked cemeteries. Living in town, it was the nearest mum and I ever got to visiting the countryside. We didn't mind. For once we were in agreement. There was nothing much to do in the country, in our combined opinions, except look. Now in a cemetery, there was weeding, watering, gravestones to read, a choice of grass, marble or bench for seating, and usually a parade of shops in walking distance of the gates.

Susan had spread her leather jacket over an old faded stone and was reading a paperback. She must have been watching out for me because she looked up when I was still some yards away. I thought back twenty years to a time when I would have run towards her and been certain of my welcome. Instead I sauntered with a careless smile glued to my face as if slightly amused by the day.

"Whew," I said peeling off mum's fur jacket, "Emotions are running high back there."

Susan laid her book face down. She stood up, took the jacket from my hands and dropped it on to the ground. Then she put her arms around me.

"That bad?" she said.

"That bad," I answered. She'd never seen me cry before.

THIRTEEN
1996
Swimming in hot water

I hate upsetting Edith. I hope I'm not becoming foolish about her, turning into a sad old thing who'll end up sending Christmas cards to all the neighbours' pets.

"Merry Xmas, Smudge and Tim Tom Cat, love and festive kippers from Edith Piaf and Joan Littler at Number 25," plus kisses and a crayoned pawmark. I know she's only a cat; but sadly, unnaturally some might say, she's still my closest friend.

Sometimes I wish I was one of those women who get on with their mothers, the 'mum and I discuss everything, more like sisters than mother and daughter' types. I mean, it's perfectly acceptable for them to say, "Oh I'll be devastated when mum dies." Everyone nods sympathetically and agrees that, "Yes, it will be an unbearable shock." The already bereaved will say, "Yes, it was an unbearable shock," and "Of course you'll never quite recover," and "I'm sure I've seen my mother at the top of the stairs and she's trying desperately to tell me something," and they'll be comforted, smothered in tissues, tea and understanding.

Now if Edith passed on, I might get a sympathetic "Oh, I am sorry, poor old you. Get a kitten-stroke-puppy immediately and a week from now I guarantee you'll have forgotten all about her."

However, if a week or so later I'm still red-eyed and muttering, "Yes, it was an unbearable shock, I'll never quite recover, and I'm sure I've seen Edith at the top of the stairs and she's trying desperately to tell me something," I'll be told not to be self-indulgent and don't I realise there are people on the other side of the world dying even as we speak.

Mum didn't encourage close family relationships, said they were an unhealthy modern phenomenon and if all the people who went on about their parents had been one of twelve brothers and sisters with the only way to recognise your mother up till the age of seven had been, "Look out for the woman in the blue hairnet," there wouldn't be so much hot air spouted on the subject.

The point of this Edith and my mother rigmarole... Actually there isn't a particular point, apart from it serving to illustrate the problem of living on one's own for several years with just a cat for company: a) you don't need a point, and b) if you have one, you aren't obliged to stick to it. Basically you can do what you want; unfortunately you find there is very little you want to do.

For 'you', read 'I'. "Own your feelings, Joan." This slogan was written with a mixture of talcum powder and toothpaste on my bathroom mirror several years ago – during a

party, in those sunny days when I was still half of a couple
and really quite popular. I never did find out who wrote it;
but now this anecdote or almost story is going to start in
earnest with Edith, crouched under the settee and refusing
to come out and get into her wicker basket.

It's hard work getting a cat out from under a settee. It's
not easy fishing a walnut out either. Lying on the ground,
my cheek pressed into the carpet, I could see Edith surrounded by several walnuts and a ping-pong ball and I
couldn't quite reach any of them. Of course I could have
moved the settee, only Edith, my main objective, would
have moved with it, and I might then have felt obliged to
get the hoover out as the settee hadn't been shifted in at
least two years. There wasn't time for hoovering or Edith's
tantrums, it was half past seven on a Saturday morning and
we should have been well on our way to Victoria Station.

We were both taking an enforced fortnight's holiday in
Mrs Botolph's Shoreham flat, thanks to my inability to
down a pint of Guinness without losing my head, and also
having become, as mum might say, 'a stranger to the truth'.
Re Mrs Botolph's flat, it had nothing to recommend it apart
from being free and sited in Shoreham, the last place anyone would think to look for me. Not that anyone would be
looking, but you – sorry I – never can tell.

The previous day I'd received a letter from Mrs B, with a
list of 'do's' and 'dont's': I would find the front door key
under the pipe-smoking gnome in the hallway, would I

please keep the newspapers in a neat pile under the television table, she would rather I didn't read them first – if I needed a newspaper there was a corner shop, and much more about stagnant milk, stale bread, and keeping the airing cupboard door closed, with a PS to on no account allow Edith on the furniture and any soiled litter must be got rid of away from the building.

So, why why was I so desperate to have Edith in her basket and the pair of us out of the area before North London began to stir? Why was it necessary to hide myself away on the South Coast? Surely Mrs Botolph's bungalow, basking in Shoreham summer sun, was hardly the most idyllic place for a fortnight away?

Trouble had been brewing; trouble had now come to the boil, all over my fabulous fictitious lover. Freddy was dynamic, Freddy was fabulous, Freddy was multi-faceted, and here lay the problem, her facets had so multiplied that I couldn't now remember who I'd told what to. Freddy was a keen angler, Freddy hated all blood sports, Freddy painted water-colours in her spare time, Freddy wrote sonnets in her spare time, Freddy had no spare time at all. She was tall; short with an authoritative manner; stocky, wiry, brown straight hair, a hint of curl, an auburn tint. Healthwise only natural remedies where Freddy was concerned, but with a childlike faith in Ibuprofen.

In the beginning I'd kept a book, subdivided pages into likes and dislikes. I'd come home, pockets full of slips of paper reminders written out in friends' toilets. "Remember Freddy is allergic to cuttlefish. Told S. Freddy only wears cotton pyjamas, later told P. Freddy sleeps in the nude."

Freddy was no longer part of my intermittent stage act – it was all too complicated. Freddy seemed real, nowadays even I almost believed in her. Since her conception I had grown more confident; in a quiet sort of way, I was even becoming quite popular. People looked in for coffee or afternoon tea, I'd given several small dinner parties. I was considering purchasing a portable barbecue, possibly a patio area. What if someone found my 'Life and Times of Freddy Fossett'? I still had the book, was fearful of throwing all that information away. Supposing one evening a curious guest marched into my kitchen between pudding and cheese courses waving it: "Sorry Joan, I was looking for some cotton wool in your chest of drawers and found this. Had to have a peep. Listen everybody." Well, I would be forced to immediately fall on the cheese knife.

In the pub, a week before, matters had come to a head. Sash and Deirdre, Penny and Jenny had already arrived. I could tell by Jenny's smug distracted air that she and Susan were still a secret item. It would all come to nothing, at least I hoped it would all come to nothing. I thought, "Penny deserves better treatment, even if she is a miserable hypochondriac with an obsession for ornamental brickwork."

Anyway I was pleased with the turn-out, and also rather pleased with my reflection in the mirror behind the bar. The top section of my head was cut off by the optics, making me look almost petite. I wore a blue chunky cotton-knit fisherman's crew which was catalogue-speak for 'summer pullover', and on one of my expensively, well-brassiered breasts, my lucky dolphin brooch bobbed gently up and down as I waved my tenner in the barmaid's direction.

"Put your money away, Joan, I'll get these." Susan clapped me on the shoulder, the warmth of her hand permeating the cotton knit. If she hadn't spoken, if I'd been standing in a bar in Paris or New York... no never mind the bar, stick me anywhere in the world and I'd have recognised Susan's hand on my shoulder. Don't misunderstand me, I wasn't still in love with her, oh no, too much water under the bridge; however, I will concede she's that one in a million women who can slump gracefully. She was slumping then, leaning forward, elbows on the top of the bar, a green crocodile-skin wallet in one tanned hand.

"God, I'm bushed," she said.

"Is that genuine crocodile skin?" I asked.

"'Fraid so," she grinned, not the slightest hint of an apology – no "A dear, long-departed friend gave it to me. I realise it may be offensive to you, Joan, with your finer sensibilities, but bear with me on this, my only memento of happier times." No, there was none of that. She was too busy admiring the wallet, flicking through her credit cards with a cheerful smile of satisfaction.

"I love plastic," she said, "beats money hands down. Remember the old days, pounds, shillings and pence. Farthings, god, how I hated farthings, and halfpennies, remember halfpennies, Joan?"

"I remember in the old days, you were a vegetarian," I said primly.

"Not possible in America, Joan. If you don't eat meat, and I mean 'eat meat', you don't fit in over there. What do you want to drink, I've asked the others?"

"A pint of Guinness, please."

"A pint of Guinnes it is then. Talking about the old days, I remember when you liked Campari and lemonade in a ladylike glass."

She turned away from me towards the barmaid who was walking towards us, smiling at Susan in particular, as if she'd found her long-lost love.

"Can you indeed? What a bloody convenient memory," I fumed as I walked slowly back to our table, allowing myself a moment to scrutinise Jenny properly and work out just why Susan preferred her company to mine. There must be more to the mystery than Jenny being younger, slimmer, prettier and better dressed. Oh, and a car driver and much travelled with some sort of degree in Italian architecture. I added good cook, connoisseur of fine wines, something of an art historian and manicured fingernails to the list as I sat down. At least Jenny had problem hair. It was at that uneasy stage between a crop and a pageboy; she was trying to tuck a long strand that had once been half of her fringe behind her ear.

"Anyone got a grip?" she asked.

"Do chemists still sell grips?" Deirdre looked brightly at the rest of us. I'd noticed this before, Deirdre's ability to ask fatuous questions in such an animated and concerned manner that everyone was forced to take the question seriously, as if we were discussing inner-city vandalism or the effects of government policy on education.

"Chemists certainly sell them in Littlehampton," I said in a confident, knowing manner that implied I could tell a few racy stories about shopping for grips.

"Who does what in Littlehampton?" This was Susan returning with our drinks. The barmaid had put them all on a circular chrome tray, an item she'd always denied having when I'd enquired.

"Grips," Sash said, "Deirdre wanted to know if they were still sold in chemists."

"Jenny wanted a grip," Penny said glumly.

"I don't need one now," Jenny reached for her drink which looked remarkably like a Campari and lemonade in a nice, ladylike glass. She sipped at it, simpered a "Thank you" in Susan's direction and then cushioned her glass in the slight depression between her two, nothing to speak of in my opinion, breasts.

Suddenly, I was grateful for my large breasts. Glad to have spent fifteen pounds that I could ill afford on my hold me up, pull me in and push me out, state-of-the-art black bra, which was just visible, straining against the stocking stitch of my jumper. I felt like Joan Sutherland in her heyday, I could have deafened the whole pub with my powerful soprano rendition of 'My Bonny Lies over the Ocean'. I thought, "Must invest in a burgundy scoop-neck T-shirt," and downed a third of my Guinness. Penny nudged my ribs,

"Susan's talking to you, Joan."

"I was asking," Susan leant across the table towards me, "When were you last actually in Littlehampton, which would bring me neatly around to enquiring after the elusive Freddy?"

Susan's expression flitted from curious to attentive to amused and back as I played for time. I polished off another third of my drink, checked my upper lip for imaginary froth. I had an overwhelming desire to touch my ears. They felt hot. Could they really be as hot as they felt?

Everyone had turned in my direction, except Jenny who was adjusting the cuffs of her corduroy trousers over the tops of her cowboy boots.

"Yes, when are we going to meet the infamous Freddy?" Sasha asked.

"When did you see her last?" Susan persisted. "You're always telling us what she's doing, but I'm never quite clear where you are in these stories."

"Well, I'm either there or I'm not there," I replied weakly. "We talk every day on the phone. Actually," my imagination rallying at last, "her mother's been in hospital for most of the summer. Touch and go really. Freddy's been torn in half between hospital, home and her horticultural practice."

"Torn in three, Joan," Susan said. I wasn't quite sure whether she was making fun of me or not.

"It must be awful for her. Is she very close to her mum?" Deirdre's voice broke with emotion.

"Very close." I looked sorrowfully into my glass. The blood was leaving my ears, they felt almost normal. I was just about to recite several unpleasant medical facts I'd gleaned from mum's *Dictionary of Organic Diseases* when Susan said, "Not meaning to be personal, Joan, but when was the last time you and Freddy got it together?"

"Got it together?" I repeated. "I don't think that's any of your business."

"That is rather a personal question, Susan," Sash said mildly.

"When was the last time any of us got it together?" Penny said morosely.

Jenny began to emery board her thumbnail. Susan was laughing, holding up her hands to ward us off, good-naturedly. Good-natured, my eye, I could see she had it in for me – I'd work out her motive later. My Guinness was finished. I took a surreptitious mouthful of Penny's neglected red wine; nobody noticed as I eased the glass in front of me.

"Look," Susan again, "I know the problems of long-distance relationships. If you don't keep stoking the fire, the fire goes out."

"Oh, very nicely put," I said.

"Joan, I'm on your side. I feel for Freddy. I love my own old mum. I'd hate anything to happen to her, bless her woolly bedsocks, but I'm concentrating on you two star-crossed lovers in this instance."

"In this instance," I repeated sarcastically. "Well thank you very much but I don't think we're in need of your concentration."

"Don't go getting on your high horse, Joan," Susan said with a smug smile.

"No Joan, don't get on your high horse, Susan's only trying to help," Deirdre pleaded as if being on a 'high horse' was a permanent position where I was concerned.

"Just listen to my suggestion, Joan," Susan continued. The whole table smiled encouragingly at me. "How about an outing to Littlehampton before winter sets in? All of us, in my Land Rover, take you both out for lunch. Pick a day next week. Now mumsy's on the mend, Fred can have a day off. I bet she's desperate to see you, Joan."

I folded my arms ready for battle. "I don't think Freddy would like a large gathering," I said.

"She'd love it. Don't worry, we wouldn't cramp your style, would we, ladies?"

They were off, all talking at once, planning the day out. How lovely, how interesting, how thrilling to meet this woman they'd all heard so much about.

"Lunch at a restaurant?"

"A pub might be more informal."

"If it's sunny, a pub with a garden would be even better."

"Is Littlehampton on the coast?"

"Yes, is Littlehampton on the coast, Joan?" Susan asked.

I hadn't a clue. I'd never ever been to Littlehampton.

I opened my mouth, closed my mouth, opened it again and said, "Actually, Freddy and I are off to Greece next week for a fortnight."

That stopped them. Not quite Susan. She exploded into a laugh which she turned into a fit of coughing.

"You're going to Greece?" Jenny laid aside her emery board. "What about Freddy's parents?"

"The council are sending in a team of carers. I didn't mention it because of Edith."

"Edith?" they all shouted.

"She's going on a farm holiday at a cattery in Waltham Abbey. She was a late booking, it's only just been confirmed."

"We would have fed her," Deirdre said.

"Thank you, but no. The place has glowing references. My customer, Mrs Porter, sends her Persians there twice a year. Edith will be fine. Freddy and I will be fine. It was a lovely, kind idea – perhaps when we get back, although I believe Freddy's starting a fairly intensive water-divining course come September. Ludicrous I know, that insatiable curiosity of hers."

I shrugged my shoulders expressively, raised Penny's glass and finished it. Deirdre promised to drop me in a Greek pocket dictionary and generously bought another round to celebrate poor Freddy's well-deserved break from tending her mother. Penny offered her *History of the Greek Islands* for holiday reading, and even Jenny said I could borrow her sarong, providing it came back washed and ironed. Only Susan was quiet, drinking slowly and steadily, ignoring Jenny's attempts to catch her attention. A couple of times I noticed her watching me, speculatively. Each time she seemed about to say something and each time I began an earnest conversation with someone else concerning wind speeds, humidity and aircraft engine failure.

I talked on and on, talked myself right up to the end of the evening. We were all pushing back our chairs, gathering together bags and jackets, saying "Goodnight," and "Happy holiday, Joan, you deserve a good one," and that favoured chestnut, "Don't do anything I wouldn't do," when Susan began chuckling to herself.

"What's the joke?" Jenny asked. She looked a little tired and sulky. "Susan, what or who are you laughing at?"

Susan shook her head, laughing even more. I'd put on my jacket, a rather nice cream linen summer weight I'd found on the men's rail in Oxfam, and was pulling at the sleeves, trying to remove some of the creases that I'd pressed in by sitting on it all evening, when Susan grabbed me by the shoulders. Her words slurring slightly, she said, "Joanie, you are an appalling person, but you never cease to amaze me," and she gave me a really good, strong hug, which after several seconds I struggled out of. I said stiffly, "I've told you before, only Freddy is allowed to call me Joanie these days," which made her laugh even louder.

Mrs Botolph had been surprisingly thoughtful. A further letter, this time written on blue Basildon Bond notepaper and sellotaped to the kettle, told me to help myself to anything I wanted within reason from her fridge-freezer.

"There's a bottle of Lambrusco chilling – Gemma tells me that's what the young are drinking these days."

"Much Gemma knows," I muttered, wasting a couple of minutes wondering just what was behind 'that's what the young are drinking these days'. I turned the sheet of paper over. "VISIT YOUR MOTHER" was written in large capitals.

Edith had also been well provided for. There were tins of

cat food, cat treats, a brand new plastic feeding dish and litter tray with a large bag of perfumed litter – no need for me
to venture out for further supplies for at least five days.

I opened the French windows and went out on to the balcony. The sea was visible behind a line of houses, an inviting hot blue. I was tempted. Early October but still warm
enough to swim and sunbathe. But no. Susan had, in mother's phraseology, 'put the wind up me'. I could tell the
Freddy question intrigued her in those quiet moments when
she wasn't holding up the traffic, petting with someone's
else's partner. Only Susan just might ask herself the question, "Where would Joan hole up for a fortnight, supposing
she wasn't really going to Greece?"

Answer: "Her mum's old friend, Mrs Botolph. Doesn't she
live in some benighted South Coast seaside town?
Shoreham-on-Sea. That's the place. Jenny, my proud beauty,
shall we go down for the day and sniff around?"

The shame and embarrassment. "Freddy and I had a serious tiff at the airport, etc, etc," was unacceptable; "Mum's
had a stroke and I rushed down here to be close, if the worst
occurred," was unpardonable, although I might just pull it
off. Better to stay put, adopt a low profile.

"If anyone knocks or rings, we're not answering," I told
Edith severely, walking back into Mrs B's lounge. Edith was
too busy testing the fitted carpet with her claws to bother
with an answer.

***

I knew the layout of the flat pretty well, although it had changed greatly from the shabby set of rooms that mum, myself, Mrs Botolph, Gemma and her new fiancé Raymond had viewed several years earlier.

We'd come down for the day; Mrs Botolph to flat-hunt, mum to visit Shepherd's Fennel Nursing Home before making a final decision, Gemma wanting to check out Shoreham's hotel situation vis à vis her wedding reception – Shoreham being her favourite spot in all the world, neither she nor Ray caring two figs for 'abroad'. Ray and I? Well Ray had to drive and I'd had nothing better to do. At the time a drive to the coast had seemed rather tempting.

The news of the 'whirlwind romance' had been brought into our kitchen the previous week by Mrs Botolph, proud grandmother, bearing Martini Bianco and a bottle of diet lemonade.

"Here's to the happy pair," she cried, having mixed the drinks and sliced up lemon at the sink as if she owned our kitchen.

"The happy pair," we'd echoed.

"Ray's really going to make something of himself in the library service."

She cut smartly across my "What exactly?" with "He won't be a librarian forever – got his eye to the future – he's into policy making."

Mum, easily impressed, whistled between her teeth admiringly.

"There'll be no more books in the future, Doll. Ray says information technology's where it's at."

"What'll happen to all the books?" Mum looked anxious. Mrs B shrugged, stared ceilingwards, "God alone knows."

"He's a technophobe, you know," she continued, refilling our glasses. I nudged mum's foot under the table to forestall another bout of whistling. "Gemma's over the moon. To be frank, she was getting a little fretful, what with her biological clock ticking away."

Mum nodded and whistled anyway.

I studied the framed photographs artistically arranged on Mrs Botolph's china cabinet and mused on how intrinsically fleeting relationships were. There was a picture of Gemma with Ray on their wedding day. She looked radiant, as pleased as Punch. 'Ray darling, Ray, precious sweetheart' stared stoically back at the camera, a 'this'll do for the time being' expression on his sharp-featured face. I still thought he'd been mad to marry her. I'd known they weren't suited after half an hour's driving on our way down to Shoreham. She'd bruised his earlobes. Squashed between Mrs B and mum, I'd watched his earlobes turn purple. I could almost feel them tingle.

"Oh, Raymondo – so many dear old Darby and Joan couples. Will we two be a loving fuddy-duddy Darby and Joan twosome, one day?"

"I have no idea who you're talking about," he'd said stiffly, dodging her fluttering hand.

She'd turned around and smiled at us, the three wise monkeys sitting silently in the back. "He works so desperately hard. Such a demanding job, isn't it sweetheart?" Her hand clasped his ear triumphantly – he shied violently away and began to overtake a container lorry at high speed.

"Settle down, Gemma," Mrs Botolph had said.

Gemma had settled down, that was obvious from a more recent photograph. She was thirty-five now. I remembered how she'd thought me forty when I was only in my late twenties – how the disparity in years lessened as one grew older.

Ray was long gone. He'd married his snooker player. Gemma's biological clock was ticking ever more slowly. No children, no partner. No longer the Gemma I recalled. This Gemma looked bone-tired – she stood with her back to the sea, smiling with a sort of desperation. Would life pick up again for her as it had eventually for me? But had it? Wasn't that just the fabrication, and in reality, wasn't I an even older, lonely woman who refused to acknowledge her unhappy situation?

"This won't do," I said, "I've only been here an hour; by six o'clock, I'll be contemplating suicide."

I'd planned the fortnight carefully. First there were practicalities to be dealt with – lists with subdivisions charted at Mrs Botolph's dining table. I'd moved on from biros to magic markers where lists were concerned – big bold lettering for big bold Joan.

Regretfully, big bold Joan's stage career wasn't going well. I needed to spend time reassessing my strengths and weaknesses – I was not yet ready for the Edinburgh Festival. Janice had advised various relaxation techniques I might use other than alcohol; she'd shown me a breathing exercise which she said would slow my pulse rate – I would become incredibly calm – and I intended to practise the exercise every morning.

So far in my short career, I'd been booed once and had a can of lager waved at me in a threatening manner, bored my audiences on at least three occasions and had two astonishing successes in small pub venues where I'd sat on the edge of a table, almost eyeball to eyeball with my audience and told tales of Freddy, mum and Edith. Afterwards, several women said I was most amusing and that they also had horticultural lovers and mums and cats remarkably like my own. I even had a one word review in *Time Out*: "Patchy."

"Patchy's good," Deirdre had said, "Patchy's not to be sniffed at. It's only a matter of evening up the evening."

"I always seem to even down the evening."

Deirdre hooted.

So, was I to be a comedienne for intimate gatherings – small parties, no more than twenty, front rooms a speciality?

My other preoccupation was all things Greece.

I'd brought Penny's *History of the Greek Islands*, and Deirdre's Greek pocket dictionary; Mrs Botolph, unlike her granddaughter, was a seasoned traveller, and had left me several brochures, a thirty-year-old phrasebook, plus a photograph album spanning several decades.

What I needed were a couple of lively anecdotes that could be repeated ad infinitum. I'd noticed regular holiday-makers did this, and it guaranteed irritation, boredom and a desire to be elsewhere in the listener.

"Petros and his wife were an adorable couple. Nothing was too good for his 'English ladies'. Did I tell you about the time he took Freddy and I out in his boat... we nearly died laughing..." Then for the smart alecs who knew every inch of Greece, I'd work on, "We went for the privacy more than anything. Most of our time was spent exercising the bed-springs." Although this wouldn't fit in with accepted Freddy folklore. Freddy was known to be an aesthete, historian and searcher out of fossils and shards of early Grecian pots. Freddy would be more likely to squat on a rock looking out to the horizon and constructing an epic poem. I could certainly turn out a fragment of an epic in a fortnight.

"Freddy wrote these. I think they're rather wonderful."

Then, and most importantly, there was my Mediterranean tan. It was late in the year, there would be storms in Greece, but I must still come back brown. Trumps again for Mrs B. Her tan creating and enhancing facilities were excellent. I had a choice of two floral upholstered sunbeds so I could follow the sun across the balcony, moving from bed to bed. Her bathroom cabinet, a giant pink melamine affair, was packed with sun cream, barrier cream, pre- and after-sun lotions and potions.

Mrs Botolph was a wonder. Her flat was so clean, squashy and comfortable. No dusty unvarnished floorboards; no brown, olive or navy; no dried flowers in vases, collecting cobwebs. Everywhere were shades of pink and cream. I sat in her bedroom, on her dressing table stool – a spindle-legged creation meant for perching daintily, not Joan's large dungareed bottom – and surveyed myself in her three-way dressing table mirror. I looked like a burglar. I smiled at my reflection. Not a bad-looking burglar.

As I mooched around the flat, my feelings regarding Mrs Botolph began to undergo a radical sea-change. For the first time in my life, I acknowledged a sneaking admiration for her. I could see what mum must have seen behind her patent snobbery and bragging – she was quite a courageous woman. She'd made a life for herself: sewing, knitting, dressmaking, painting bad flower pictures, amateur photography. I found books on table etiquette and how to make the perfect cocktail, running a country hotel and *Bee-keeping – A cottage industry*. What a pity the Wing Commander had died. She'd have been a perfect hostess at RAF parties, teasing the men in her awkward, heavy way, and amusing and smoothing their wives' feathers.

During my first tanning session on the balcony, I thought a good deal about Mrs Botolph, mum and Mrs Scott, and very little about my non-existent career. After my second Martini, lemonade and a slice of lemon, I came to a conclusion: Mrs Botolph was a lesbian. Because of education and upbringing she had no idea she was a lesbian – any sexual fantasies she might have had were sidetracked into the love and caring she'd given to her women-friends. I would write about them all. At some point in the future, I'd change their names, subtly alter their characters. A script for radio or television. I was excited. The sun went down and it grew chilly. I came inside, sat in Mrs Botolph's comfortable Parker Knoll armchair, her tin of chocolate bourbons and bag of knitting at my feet. I felt a rush of warm affection for her.

Why, one day, I'd surprise everybody, but I wouldn't think about surprising everybody, time enough for that when I'd written something.

FOURTEEN
First draft

Dolly Littler and Mrs Scott sat in wheelchairs; Mrs Botolph (christened "our twice-weekly visitor from outer space" by Dolly) overflowed on to a red plastic chair. She'd brought in a cushion from home to make herself more comfortable but it was invisible beneath the box pleats of her smart gabardine skirt.

"Well, I don't know how I'm going to last out the day," she grumbled, "That damn machine's still not working. Have you got any, Dolly?"

"Look in my bag." Dolly nudged her large leather bag in Mrs Botolph's direction with her foot.

"I don't like going through another woman's handbag," said Mrs Botolph, picking it up from the floor and starting to rummage, "Whatever are you doing with old electricity and gas bills?"

"I work out my anagrams in the margins."

"Can't Joan bring you in some scrap paper?"

"Joan fusses. She'll say, "Colour preference, size, lined, unlined, envelopes to match? Everything's a bloody production – she drives me mad."

"You're a lucky beggar. There's two packets of twenty in here."

Dolly smirked, "Conscience cigarettes. Joan brings them in on her once-in-a-blue-moon visit."

"I'm surprised they don't frisk her at the door, she looks like a drug smuggler with that headband. What's eight down?"

"The old Manx cat makes too much noise. Six letters."

Dolly sucked on her biro, while Mrs Botolph blew smoke thoughtfully into the air. Mrs Scott's head nodded forward and she seemed to sleep. Her fingers had been tightly clenched in her lap; now they slowly uncurled. Dolly thought what pretty hands Mrs Scott still had. If she was only shown Mrs Scott's hands and asked to describe a possible owner, she would have said, "A young woman with soft fair hair. Loved by someone, with a toddler or two. Probably rides a bike."

"Penny for them, Doll?" Mrs Botolph came down from her smoke clouds.

"I was thinking what young hands Mrs Scott has. There's something of the water lily about them."

Mrs Botolph rested her fuchsia-painted fingertip in the centre of Mrs Scott's upturned palm. The fingers snapped tight around it like a Venus flytrap. Mrs Scott's eyes opened a fraction.

"Marvellous reflexes still," said Dolly as Mrs Botolph removed her finger gently and patted Mrs Scott's arm.

The Coffee Shop was a new innovation at the nursing home, made from two attics knocked into one large room with dormer windows, sliding doors and a balcony leading to a fire escape, which no resident was to be allowed on unless accompanied by a member of staff.

It was coming to the final days of a trial run: two weeks of opening ten to twelve and two-thirty to four-forty-five. The forthcoming Saturday heralded the official naming ceremony. Mrs Deirdre Flood JP would not only cut a ribbon and an iced sponge cake, but also award a two-pound box of Milk Tray and a bouquet of late spring flowers to whichever resident had come up with the most appropriate name.

So far, interest had been tepid, the list on a piece of A4 card, adjacent to the Menu Board, was dominated by suggestions from Dolly and Mrs Botolph.

"You'll never get anywhere with 'Ye Olde Sheep Dip', Dolly."

"That was meant to be a joke."

"You want the Milk Tray, don't you?" Mrs Botolph asked.

"I'm not bothered. Madame's probably rigged the whole caboodle in any case."

"Shh," said Mrs Botolph, and nodded her head towards the food hatch where Meg, 'Madame's' daughter sat reading on an upturned milk crate.

'Madame', the owner, was a tall woman of haughty manner and a double-barrelled name – no one was quite certain of its pronunciation. Madame had a habit of slurring her words which Dolly and Mrs Botolph claimed to be the sign of the impeccable thoroughbred, while Joan insisted it was nothing more than the sign of an inveterate tippler.

"For heavens sake, mum, the veins on her nose and cheeks, they're engorged."

Dolly had said, "I don't like that word, actually, Joan, and those veins indicate a life in the open air; hunting, shooting and Cowes Week."

"That doesn't necessarily preclude a drink problem."

"Preclude, what sort of word is 'preclude', Joan?"

"Debar, exclude – eight letters."

Not that Dolly or Mrs Botolph liked Madame. On the contrary, they absolutely disliked her but they wouldn't let Joan know that. They united against Joan. Agreed all Joan's reactions were based on airy-fairy theories of class, picked up from her ill-dressed, mis-informed new friends in London. As Dolly said, "Joan has always been gullible. She finds a different guru every five years or so."

Mrs Botolph, not for the first time, had been impressed. Dolly, for all her drab clothes and ineptitude at crossword puzzles, often surprised her. She would have liked to ask how she came by the word 'guru', and used it with such confidence, when she led such a secluded life, but that would have meant Mrs Botolph having to step down from her own stylish pedestal; an action quite unthinkable for both of them.

Each Tuesday and Friday, Mrs Botolph visited, coming on the train from Shoreham, arriving in time for lunch and going home just before the staff gathered their flock in for dinner at six o'clock.

"Who eats dinner at six o'clock in the evening? Especially in the summer months?" Mrs Botolph remonstrated.

"We're not a sophisticated lot here, Mrs B. We need topping and tailing and commode chairs emptying before being tucked up for the night. 'Eat early – less accidents,' that's Matron's maxim. It wouldn't do for you," Dolly said.

"It most certainly wouldn't," Mrs Botolph agreed. She lowered her voice, "And I'd have something to say about yon miss read-ing novels all day long."

"She borrows them off the residents. Sometimes they're left behind by the dead," Dolly said ghoulishly.

They both pulled faces and watched Meg covertly. She was halfway through 'Forever Amber', and not to be disturbed. Mrs Botolph had been forced to organise their three weak teas and Cherry Bakewells herself.

"Work experience before Sussex University," Dolly whispered.

Meg looked up from her book, "Whispering is rude," she said severely.

"Mrs Scott's asleep," said Mrs Botolph with an insincere smile, "Twenty-four across, Dolly?"

" 'It's played with spirit to a stormy conclusion.' Five letters. We're not doing very well."

Mrs Scott opened her eyes and smiled a gentle, lost smile. She began tapping her hands up and down, up and down on the arms of her wheelchair.

"If this place caught fire," Dolly said, lighting a cigarette, "Mrs Scott and I would be roasted alive in these wheelchairs. You and Meg would be all right. You could both scoot down the fire escape. It would be like 'Towering Inferno', with no Frank Newcombe to save us."

Mrs Scott, an ardent film-goer in healthier days, stirred irritably.

"Paul Newman. Why do you tease her so, Dolly?"

"Keeps her on her toes. You're all there really, aren't you?" Dolly shook the arm of Mrs Scott's wheelchair, "Want a fag? Mrs Botolph, put 'Towering Inferno' on the list, and 'The Jolly Fire Hazard' as well."

Mrs Botolph heaved herself off the chair and rearranged her pleats before lumbering across to the poster.

Meg was finally aroused, "Now Mrs Botolph, if you put fire in people's minds, they'll make this place 'No Smoking', then you and Mrs Littler will be stuck. It'll be back to winter puffing on the patio and you both had bronchitis last year."

"You're a sensible girl, Meg." Mrs Botolph added, "But idle," under her breath.

"I've written 'Old Scottie's Retreat', and 'The Ring of Roses Tearoom," she told Dolly. "If it's only you and me on the list, one of us has to win."

"You'll be disqualified," Dolly said, "you're not a resident."

Mrs Botolph sat down again and leant across the table conspiratorially, "Not if everyone keeps their mouths shut. Madame doesn't know B from a bull's foot about who is and who isn't a resident here, and Matron and the nurses won't give me away, I've greased too many palms in the past."

They chattered on, tossing possible names across the table, chuckling, waking Mrs Scott and making her chuckle, a funny sharp cluck, like a very old hen. Mrs Botolph folded away their newspapers and produced a pack of cards. They played Snap, and Dolly became warm and over-excited and had to take off her cardigan. Mrs Scott was given a hand of cards which she stared at brightly, before drifting away somewhere and letting the cards slither to the floor.

At a quarter to five, their favourite nurse came in to take Mrs Scott downstairs and both Mrs Botolph and Dolly hissed playfully at her. Meg hid 'Forever Amber' underneath the till and said, "The three of them have been extremely disruptive today."

As a rule, Mrs Botolph went shopping in Worthing town centre on Saturday mornings; but the Saturday of the Grand Opening she dressed with care, as befitted a possible prize winner, or the friend of a possible prize winner. She had a faint recollection of Deirdre Flood JP, from various WRVS functions she'd attended since moving to the South Coast. She recalled a smart woman in her sixties who favoured navy worn with white patent shoulder bag and shoes. Mrs Botolph considered the advisability of wearing a pair of light summer gloves, but decided against as a) they would conceal her beautifully manicured hands, b) they would conceal her very fine collection of dress rings and c) Dolly's awful daughter Joan would be coming with her shabby London sophistication and a new girlfriend in tow. She could imagine the sly glances she'd get from Joan as she stored patronising little details of the event to get mileage from during her drugs- and sex-filled winter evenings in Hackney. Almost any unpleasant event she read about in her newspaper that concerned North London, she imagined Joan or her ilk had a hand in it.

But now was not the time for musing on Joan's wrong-doings, instead she admired her imposing figure in the long mirror of her imposing flame mahogany double wardrobe. Very nice. Life had never been better since she'd grown stout. The stouter she became, the more respect she seemed to inspire.

"The secret," she thought, "is to combine the extra weight with being impeccably dressed."

She'd explained her theory to her granddaughter Gemma, when she'd put on weight after Raymond left her for the buxom younger Peggy from the Snooker Club.

"Don't worry about weight. Any man worth his salt can happily cope with a stone or two of extra flesh – or else he's not a real man."

For a moment Mrs Botolph's complacency slipped. It was a pity Gemma wanted a real man – it was her mother's doing – neither had been ones for girlfriends. Her painted smile wavered, and she wondered at the value of winning a two-pound box of chocolates that she could easily afford to buy, and rubbing shoulders with a JP. What did it all matter? Then she remembered Dolly and Mrs Scott. She really was very fond of them – particularly Dolly, who'd filled gaps when life was grey. She patted a little more powder beneath her eyes, squirted Youth Dew on the inside of each braceleted wrist and set off for the station.

Red, white and blue bunting fluttered in the breeze from the stately white pillars of Shepherd's Fennel Nursing Home. The windows on the ground floor were open to welcome in the fresh morning air.

In the gardens, bees hummed relentlessly, moving lazily between clumps of lavender backed by tall maroon and pink hollyhocks. On the lawn, white plastic tables and chairs had been set out in inviting clusters. Madame and Matron patrolled the exterior of the building, checking all was in order before their guests arrived.

"Possibly a cup of coffee in the shade?" Madame suggested, "It's so much quieter out here, we can actually hear ourselves think. And there's the names of the Coffee Shop Competition to sort out."

While Matron went in search of coffee, Madame sat down in the shade of an elderly laburnum tree. She took a dog-eared piece of card from her slim leather briefcase and studied it with an expression of distaste. She was still frowning as Matron padded across the lawn carrying a loaded tin tray.

"I never take biscuits in the morning," Madame said, "and absolutely no sugar. How are things indoors?"

"Moving along nicely. We're nearly all washed and dressed. The first visitors should start coming in about eleven. There'll be the Brighton train and then the London. There's room in the car park for eight cars and I've cordoned off an area for Mrs Flood's Peugeot."

"Good, good," Madame stirred her coffee morosely. There was a sharp tapping on an upstairs window. They both started, and squinted upwards.

"It's Dolly Littler," Matron said. She turned her chair slightly, to better see Dolly, who was mouthing something through the glass, making exaggerated movements of her face.

"Should we just ignore her?" Madame asked.

"Oh no, Dolly's very compos mentis… Laburnum's a what?" Matron shouted.

Dolly mouthed again and Matron nodded, "She says 'Laburnum's a killer'. She's talking about the tree we're sitting under. Actually, taken internally, laburnum can be unpleasant."

"Better put a sign up then. Now this list of names. Is it some sort of a joke?"

"Some of our residents are still capable of jokes," said Matron, smiling.

"Well, I don't find this joke amusing. We have Deirdre Flood arriving here in less than two hours, and all we've got is this non-sense to show her."

" 'The Ring of Roses Tearoom' is passable."

"But where is the relevance?" Madame was becoming annoyed, "There are no roses at Shepherd's Fennel. This is a rose-free nursing home. Insurance cover demands it."

The Coffee Shop was crowded. A small stage had been set up at the back of the room, the tables were folded away against the walls and plastic chairs were arranged in rows behind a front row of occupied wheelchairs. Dolly had chosen to come on foot for a change, leaning heavily on Mrs Botolph's arm. They'd come up early, primarily to secure seats at the end of the second row – to make their access to the stage easier, but also to avoid having to talk for too long to Joan and ner new girlfriend, Freddy. Mrs Scott snoozed peacefully in her wheelchair. Dolly poked her sharply in the back. She jerked awake and muttered, "Stop it, Scottie."

"She's on form today," Dolly said.

"I think your Joan could have made more of an effort. Why must she bring these waifs and strays with her? They all dress as if they've just come in from digging the garden," Mrs Botolph said disagreeably.

"Joan never could bear her own company. This new one's got a rather pleasant face – she's a local girl – Littlehampton."

"Looks more like a local boy."

Joan and Freddy were standing together by an open dormer window. Joan wore baggy cotton trousers, a loose, washed-out T-shirt, her hair tied back in a ponytail with an Indian headband showing beneath her fringe. Freddy was in tight denim workwear and motorcycle boots. Joan waved cheerfully at Dolly and Mrs Botolph – Dolly smiled, Mrs Botolph sniffed and looked away.

The room was hot, even with all the windows open. The French windows leading to the fire escape remained firmly closed. "We can't afford accidents," Madame had said earlier.

There were people standing in the doorway, a crowd stretching back to the lift and stairwell. Meg, positioned at the front of the room, which had now become the back of the room, switched on a portable record player and Harry Secombe singing 'If I Ruled the World' blasted out.

Madame, who had changed into a grey silk dress, fought her way through the crowd to her daughter.

"Quieter, Meg, quieter, and watch for my signal. Have we nothing more melodic?"

Meg looked blank, then hostile, "These are all Harry Secombe," she said, "It's all there was. It's not my fault."

"No hymns?" Madame asked hopefully. Meg raised her eyes heavenwards and began flipping through the pile of records. "And watch for my signal," Madame headed for the stage again.

"I'm watching, I'm watching."

"Such a pleasure and an honour to open this venture, which I hope," Deirdre Flood clapped her summer-gloved hands together, "which I know, will be a success. I see this dear little tearoom becoming the beating heart of the nursing home."

She paused and there was a spattering of polite clapping.

"Well, I've cut the ribbon and in a few moments we'll all partake of a small slice of this delicious cake," she waved towards the two-tiered sponge drooping on a small occasional table brought up from the Lounge, "but first the naming ceremony. I

believe Matron has been inundated with suggestions."

Matron handed her a small lilac envelope.

Dolly leaned forward, her hands clutching the back of Mrs Scott's wheelchair. Mrs Botolph breathed deeply to calm her racing heart. The cellophane wrapping of the two-pound box of Milk Tray gleamed invitingly; in a red fire bucket, a bouquet of freesias, gypsophila and lilies waited.

"And the prize-winning name is 'The Chardonnay', and we have Mrs Patricia Scott to thank for her suggestion."

To a round of enthusiastic applause, Matron moved briskly from the makeshift podium and took hold of Mrs Scott's wheelchair, whizzing her towards Deirdre Flood.

"Congratulations, my dear," Deirdre Flood kissed her on both cheeks and the box of chocolates was rested in her lap. Mrs Scott smilled, and then as the flowers were placed in her lifeless arms she began to cry and shake her head.

"Yes, they are yours," Deirdre Flood smiled at the audience, "Bless her, she's quite overcome."

Madame moved forward, still clapping in a polite affected way, and murmured, "Matron, I think you'd better take her back downstairs."

She nodded towards Meg sitting on the counter of the serving hatch. "Sandwiches, cakes and tea are being served outside on the lawns. If we could make our way smoothly out." Harry Secombe drowned: "And thank you so much for your support."

Joan and Freddy sprawled on the grass; Dolly and Mrs Botolph rested in garden chairs; Mrs Scott and her prizes had been confined to her bedroom.

"It's a bloody sauce," said Mrs Botolph.

"It was only a bit of fun, wasn't it?" said Freddy, through a salad sandwich.

"Not to me, it wasn't."

"We didn't really expect to win, did we?" asked Dolly.

"I did. My two were the only half-sensible suggestions. I've a good mind to contact the local paper. It would make a ruddy good story, woman JP and nursing home involved in fraud."

"Mrs Scott will share the chocolates with you anyway."

"It's the winning that counts, Joan," Mrs Botolph said.

"I don't know why you want to sit up there. I felt quite claustrophobic, didn't you, Freddy?"

"Give me wide open spaces," Freddy laid her hand over Joan's. Mrs Botolph and Dolly fell silent and Dolly gave Mrs Botolph one of her 'See what I've had to put up with' glances. Dolly said, "Whatever you think, Joan, this is our home, and we can choose to sit where we want. It doesn't have to have your approval."

"But mum. It's unhealthy being indoors all day, and with all due respect," her tone became sarcastic, "it's not Mrs Botolph's home. I'm surprised at you, Mrs Botolph, you used to be a sun worshipper." Joan reached for another sandwich, lifted the top slice, peered inside and said, "I won't even ask what this brown paste is."

Dolly watched them all leave from the Lounge window. Joan and Freddy climbing into a red van, 'Fossett's Horticultural Services' signwritten on the side. Mrs Botolph ahead of them, not *waving, limping slightly, the shopping bag she'd brought to carry home winners' chocolates swinging against her bad leg.*

Behind Dolly in the Lounge, the television was already switched on, but not loudly, and there wasn't the usual level of noise. Dolly wondered if she should look in on Mrs Scott, only she felt very tired.

"It will pass," she said to herself.

She sat in her armchair, next to Mrs Scott's empty armchair, and opened the thin envelope Joan had left for her. It was always the same: four large crosswords, cut from Joan's Friday evening newspaper. Even so, she turned the envelope upside down and shook it.

TAPE 4

Q: Was that story true?
Joan: Some of it. Madame did rig the competition so that Mrs Scott won. Obviously Freddy's a figment.
Q: Wasn't Mrs Botolph going to be a lesbian?
Joan: Mrs Botolph was an absolute bugger. Even as a quasi-fictional character she fought lesbianism every step of the way.
Q: So that was a draft of...?
Joan: Episode one of the series. Initially I wrote the whole thing as prose stories. In the next episode, all becomes clear in flashback. I could control Mrs B better once I'd changed her name to Mrs Dunbarton.
Q: Will she recognise herself?
Joan: Oh yes.
Q: Won't she be annoyed?
Joan: I expect so.

FIFTEEN
Toughening up

"Home at last, Edith."

She'd put on weight in Shoreham, the cat basket weighed a ton. I lowered it on to the floor and unlatched its door. Not much movement. One malevolent green eye opened, then closed again accompanied by a deep, world-weary sigh.

While we'd been away I'd learned something fresh about Edith's character. She was a snob: a cat who approved of thick pile carpets, pastel-coloured mohair throws and a sunny balcony with a fresh sandy litter tray – she didn't want to re-accustom herself to bare boards and a complete absence of pink or palest ecru in my decor.

"We must toughen up," I said, shaking her basket so she fell out in an undignified heap. She followed me into the kitchen where we both settled at the kitchen window and stared morosely at storm clouds and driving rain – I was dubious about Edith re-accustoming herself to a wet muddy bottom.

A word about my 'bare boards'. These do not form fashionable flooring. They've not been sanded and polished and strewn with expensive ethnic rugs. They are just old floorboards patterned in places with paint and ink-blots from my various cheap fountain pens.

I do have a couple of rugs. 'Heirlooms', mum says. One circular, one oval, plaited from pairs of mum's nylons during the 1950s; made before she had a television, or became interested in vocabulary. They'd worn remarkably well, still the same mixtures of brown, tan and off-white – not Mrs Botolph's style at all.

I left my suitcase in the hall just in case of social calls, 'Zakynthos to Gatwick' on the prominent luggage labels, artfully creased by me to imply heavy usage in transit. I wanted a cup of tea but mixed myself an Ouzo instead.

"I've got so used to Ouzo. Freddy and I can't get enough of the stuff." I sat down on the bottom stair and played back my telephone messages. Nine. I'd never had nine calls registering before.

1. Janice. "Long time no see or hear, Joan." She was organising a Festival of Women's Voices, would I fill an eight-minute slot between a soprano from Cwmbran and selections from *Jane Eyre – The Musical* performed by Moira Gunnings. "Joan, Moira must not be missed," Janice finished with.

2. Deirdre and Sash offering me any weekend for the next six months if only I'd bring along Freddy and our holiday snaps. "We love looking at other women's holiday snaps." Were they mad?

3. "Why didn't you visit your mother? You were hardly a stone's throw away. Joan, you've never failed to

disappoint me. There are cat hairs on my bathrobe."

4,5,6. Work. Work. Work.

7. "I'm absolutely distraught," Jenny.

8. "I'm absolutely destroyed," Penny.

Finally a vaguely familiar, quiet voice. "I hope we're still friends... I couldn't think of anyone else to talk to... who knew me well enough... Rachel feels Persephone needs a father. She says she's tired of living on the outside... met a man at work who's kind and caring. They're getting married. I can hardly..." and the tape ran out.

I sipped my drink thoughtfully. No, I didn't like Ouzo. I couldn't imagine Freddy doting on it either. I poured it down the sink and filled up the kettle, all the time still thinking about Steff – not that self-absorbed half of a couple at the party the previous year, but the one I remembered from years ago, the woman who'd always made time for other people. Steff was special. How could Rachel be so cold-blooded?

I riffled through my address book, searching out the number I'd sworn I'd never ring and then, my hand hovering over the receiver, suddenly, surprisingly, my reflection in the hall mirror made me pause.

I realised I hadn't taken off my hat. It was wide-brimmed, made of straw with a turquoise paisley bandanna tied around the crown. I'd chosen it while in Shoreham because it looked most like a hat I might buy in Greece. I tipped it back, bringing my face out of the shadow of the brim. I looked well and content; a smooth tan with a touch of healthy pink on my cheekbones, freckles across the bridge of my nose. I approved of that face in the mirror. No great beauty but not bad at all.

"Don't just jump in, Joan," I said to her, "Think a little first. You've come a long way – try not to retrace your steps." I couldn't quite smile at my solemn face.

Under my hand the telephone rang. Automatically I lifted the receiver.

"Thank God you're back, Joan. I thought you were coming home yesterday."

"Yes Jenny, I had a lovely holiday. How are you?"

"Dreadful. Did you get my message? Has Penny got to you, yet? Of course you've always been more her friend than mine…"

"What are you talking about?"

"We're splitting up. It's over. She wants me to buy her out."

"Buy her out?"

"Of the house. Her half. Or she'll buy me out. I can't bear it. I love that house," she began to wail loudly.

"Matters have moved rather rapidly in a fortnight, haven't they?" I said. "You both seemed perfectly happy when I went away."

"You're not observant, Joan. We were anything but happy. I'm not getting any younger," pause for much angry nose-blowing, "Penny is not the be-all and end-all of my life. Oh no. I set my sights a little higher, I hope."

"I like Penny."

"Everyone likes Penny. Liking someone won't carry me

through to old age."

"What or who will then?" I asked, irrelevantly recalling mum telling me that 'love buttered no parsnips', after Susan left.

"I'm in love with Susan. I've always been in love with her, ever since we first met."

I almost said, "Join the club, what makes you think you're so special?" Instead I said, "I know."

"You do?" The nose-blowing stopped.

"Yes. I saw you both together in Islington."

"Well I can tell by your tone that you don't approve."

"It's none of my business what you do. I don't want to see Penny hurt, that's all."

"Bully for Penny. What about me?" Jenny's voice rose angrily, "What Susan wants Susan gets – then once she's got it she doesn't want it any more."

My spirits began to flutter upwards, "Are you saying, Susan doesn't want you?"

"Susan has gone to Spain with that ridiculous Angel Baby and her mother, yet I know she loved me."

I had a vision of Susan and that woman, both in evening dress, driving along in an old-fashioned tourer-style car, Angel Baby in the back; evening scarves, Angel's long hair, all flying behind them in the warm Spanish breeze.

"Did she say how long she'd be gone?"

"She said, 'As long as it takes.' As long as what takes? The dust to settle, the pair of them and their woman child to build a cosy adobe hacienda, for pigs to start flying?"

"Oh dear," I said.

"Oh dear is insufficient. My life's ruined, boats burnt. I need to come around and talk it through with someone who knew Susan."

"The kettle's boiling."

"Sod the kettle. I'll bring a bottle. I must have a drink."

"No. You can't come," I said firmly, "At the moment I have my own problems. Freddy and I... look, I've got to go." I hadn't the energy left to embark on another Freddy anecdote, I needed tea and a hot-water bottle.

Outside the rain was now torrential, ideal weather for desperate women, not the Susans of this world who pack up and move to a warmer climate as soon as the going gets rough.

"I think I'm getting flu," I told the teapot. God, I must stop talking to cats and inanimate objects.

Huddled into the corner of the settee, a blanket over my knees, hot-water bottle clasped against my stomach, I finally acknowledged the secret I'd even kept hidden from myself.

Jenny and Susan hadn't really bothered me. Nor Angel Baby – not deep down. I'd known Susan was safe with them. They wouldn't touch her, not like I had in the past. I'd allowed myself to nurture hopes. Daydreams of tanned and laughing Joanie swanning into the pub looking ten years younger with her carefully prepared Freddy nonsense. Susan not absolutely sure it was nonsense, but anyway intrigued. I'd thought, just give me the chance and I can swing it. I've

learnt to check my exuberance; I could be cool or passionate, hadn't I served my apprenticeship? "Maybe this time…"
I was Liza Minnelli as Sally Bowles, a courageous loser who
might have changed her run of bad luck.

I didn't cry. I went to bed and willed myself not to think.
In the morning I worked through my calls, my diary open
on my knees. I told Mrs Botolph I'd had bronchitis, I was on
antibiotics, and managed several realistic hacking coughs.
She said, "I'm surprised there's not more phlegm, Joan." I
told Deirdre that Freddy and I were having problems;
Freddy had developed a nervous sciatica on the plane out
and proved an irritable invalid – we were reconsidering our
relationship. Penny was out; Steff I put off calling until later
in the week when I'd had time to toughen up.

SIXTEEN
1997
An isolated beauty

"Honestly, Steff," Jenny drawled, "I've had to resort to cigarettes just to hang on to my sanity. Can you believe I've been reduced to this?" She waved a dismissive hand at my garden in all its shimmering autumn opulence.

"I think it's very good of Joan to put you up indefinitely," Steff said. She was stretched out in the deckchair next to mine.

"Oh, I pay my way," Jenny's voice became brittle and defensive, "My money keeps our budding playwright in pens and paper."

"You pay your rent, Jenny. I still have to go out gardening three days a week and it's bloody hard work this time of year, with all the pruning. Do stop pacing up and down – there's another deckchair in the shed."

"No thank you. I can't sit down, I'm too full of unspent energy."

Steff and I exchanged weary glances. I shrugged, half-closed my eyes and turned my face sunwards.

"Couples are deadly," Jenny droned on, "they become

clones of one another, lose all individuality. I've had it with chinos and white silk socks; jewel-like colours for me in the future, and tactile fabrics."

Her lighter clicked as she lit another of her pink cigarettes, "In this ephemeral stage between youth and middle-age, I want to be... a butterfly."

"For god's sake," Steff snapped, "Why can't you just be an intelligent grown woman for half an hour?"

"Because I've done that and look where I've ended up."

She arced her cigarette into the flowerbed and walked away, dead-heading any perfectly healthy geranium in her path.

"I don't know how or why you put up with her."

"She's not all bad," I said, hoping Steff wouldn't ask me to name one redeeming feature. "The money is handy."

"Hah," Steff said.

It was almost exactly two years now, since I'd been to Steff and Rachel's flat for the first time. I hardly recognised Steff, her face swollen from continuous crying, hair lank and unwashed. She led me into the kitchen – a bright and cheerful room covered with a thin layer of recent dust.

"Only chamomile," she said, putting on the kettle, "The milk's sour."

"I'd have brought some in, if you'd said." Immediately I thought how trivial that sounded, I hadn't come for the polite ritual of afternoon tea and cake. I sat at their pine table, facing the family pinboard – several vivid childish drawings, leaflets for Kew and the Chelsea Physic Gardens, two postcards of Vera Brittain, a view of the Cairngorms – I searched for the Ivy Compton-Burnett, "It is better to be drunk and beat the ground than let the deeper things escape." It was gone. Had Rachel taken it with her to impress some other poor victim?

"So how are you, Joan? How's your mother?"

"We're both fine. She'll get a telegram from the Queen at the rate she's going."

"What rate's that?"

"Slow but sure."

Steff wasn't really listening. Next to the kettle stood a small jam-jar full of dying asters; their purples and pinks fading away to a papery brown. She stared down at them, feathering her fingers across the fringe of dry petals.

"Persephone picked them for me… from his garden," she said quietly.

"Have you met him?"

"He seems very nice. Warm and sympathetic. He'll make a good father."

"But what about you? Surely you have rights?"

She poured water into flowered mugs and the heavy smell of chamomile filled the room.

"Apparently very few. We never put anything in joint names. Rachel's her mother – the name on the Birth Certificate. We'd planned a ceremony for one day in the future; there's a wild and beautiful place we know in the Lake District. All our friends would be there, singing, dancing. We were going to exchange vows – the three of us, at a time when Persephone would be old enough to appreciate the significance of what we were sharing."

Had it been two other women's overheard conversation, I would have shouted, "Stuff and bloody nonsense," only it was our conversation, and even I, as self-absorbed as I was at that time with my own problems, couldn't fail to see how catastrophic this particular parting was.

"What I wondered," Steff said, "Could you be here, when Rachel comes to collect the last of their things? I can't face it."

"Of course," I said automatically.

"Don't be rude to her. I know you're capable of it, Joan. I'd like them to believe I was perfectly sanguine to the idea that it is for the best."

"You're mad. You should fight."

"And then what? The two of us screaming down the telephone, the solicitors' letters, court appearances – what would that do to Persephone? If I'm reasonable, I'll still see her sometimes."

Nothing I could say would change her mind. Perhaps she was right. Right or wrong, sanguine or angry, it made no difference to Rachel and warm sympathetic Jim.

"I'm so glad Steff's got you, Joan," Rachel said. It was two days later and I was back in their – no, Steff's – kitchen, standing face to face with Rachel while Jim, his head sunk between his shoulders, carried boxes and cases out to a hired box van.

"She hasn't 'got me'. I'm not stepping in again as you step out. Don't try and ease your conscience that way."

"I meant, I'm glad there's a friend here for her."

"Very noble," I sneered.

"I couldn't help falling in love," she said defensively.

"Again?"

"Jim's very different. Steff and I were two equals; Jim and I are the two matching halves of an apple."

I was speechless for once, staring down this ex–shadow-woman who'd changed considerably in the intervening years. Gone was the pale face and long, untidy hair; she wore make-up now – too much – like someone unused to wearing it. Her hair was swept up at the back of her head into a glossy pleat – tendrils escaping each side of her face. The adoring Jim in the background, puffing and panting; attractive, youthful Mr and Mrs with daughter – Mrs Botolph would approve.

"And won't it break Persephone's heart?"

"It's better in the long run." She paused and looked slightly embarrassed. "She won't be Persephone any more. It's too blatant. We thought Ruth or Meg. One syllable – keep it simple. She deserves a normal childhood."

My fists clenched but I thought, "Get them out of the house, Joan. That's what you're here for. Avoid punching her on the nose if you can."

"Penny for them, Joan," Steff said.

I blinked, my eyes focusing on the garden devoid of Jenny.

"She's gone," Steff said, "an offer of a party and a shared bed for the weekend in affluent Primrose Hill."

"Good riddance. Peace at last." I sighed, "I'm visiting mum tomorrow."

"Can I come? I haven't seen your mum in years."

"Better not. Mrs Botolph may be there. She's only recently begun looking at me with a benign eye, I don't want to spoil her mood. How about dinner on Sunday?"

Steff fiddled with a blade of glass as if deep in thought, her sadness palpable.

"Normally Pers... Ruth rings me on Sundays, but they're all away in Scotland at the moment. I'm so used to being home waiting for her call."

"Tell you what," I said coaxingly, "we could make jam."

She laughed then, "No Joan, I've looked in your larder, you've enough jam to last you for years, but dinner would be lovely."

Mum had had her eighty-eighth birthday the week before. To me, it seemed she'd been old for so many years, it was hard to judge just how old she now looked. Her conversation was still as sharp and witty, but I'd begun to suspect more and more of it was fictional.

"Happy birthday for Tuesday," I said loudly, sweeping into her room with presents, several newspapers and my rucksack weighed down with apples.

"I've brought you fresh produce," I said.

She looked up reluctantly from her book, squinted

behind her spectacles to bring me into focus, "I wish you wouldn't. Madame won't thank you for it."

"Did you get my card?"

"Yes."

"And?"

"And it didn't amuse me in the least. I don't like mucky humour."

I dropped my bags on the floor, and went to look at myself in her cheval mirror. Her mirror was more flattering than the one I had at home; in it, I looked almost slim.

"You're getting fat," mum said.

"I am not," I said, "What's the book?"

"*Anna Karenina*."

"Aren't you still doing the puzzles?"

"I've given up puzzles. I'm working my way through the foreign classics."

"What else have you read?" I asked, piling her presents neatly at the end of the bed to be opened after I'd gone – one of our rituals, as Sandy Banks might have said.

"*Papillon*."

"That's hardly a foreign classic."

"It's a very good read."

"Is it?" I looked down at her curly grey head and felt an overwhelming desire to hug her, which wouldn't have been appreciated in the least. "There's a glamorous bed-jacket in one of those packets, don't let Madame get her hands on it."

"She won't want bed-jackets. There's a lover involved."

I straightened up from building an apple pyramid in the

centre of a crocheted doily, "What? Are you sure? She's married."

Mum gave me a withering look, "You can have a lover and be married."

"How do you know about this lover? I can't see her broadcasting it around the nursing home."

"He's one of the inmates."

"There's not a man under eighty with his own set of teeth in here. Not a man under eighty, for that matter."

"Teeth can do a lot of damage in a sexual relationship," mum said mysteriously.

"I thought you didn't like 'mucky'."

"There's 'mucky' and 'mucky'."

"Is Mrs Botolph coming in?"

"Not today. She sends her regards and says when will that play you've written about her be on the radio? She'd like advance warning, so she can alert her neighbours."

"It's not exactly about her. Artistic licence, mum. Anyway, it's not a radio play, it's a television series and still in the planning stage. Contracts haven't been signed."

"Am I in it?"

"Sort of," I said uneasily, "I changed your name to Dottie Fisher."

I met Madame on the way out, swishing along in a navy crêpe de Chine sleeveless dress. I searched her face and bare arms for signs of passionate gumming – nothing – as always, her make-up was immaculate.

"How is your mother?" she asked regally, as if I were the resident and mum the visitor.

"She seems all right. What do you think?"

"I'm Administration, Joan. Between ourselves, I couldn't cope if I had anything whatsoever to do with our clients' physical or mental welfare. I should go ga-ga."

We fell into slow step together, walking down the lino-tiled hall towards the umbrella and walking-stick stand and giant plastic yucca.

"However, Matron does say your mother is 'all there'," she tapped her forehead with an elegant index finger, "which is refreshing. Most of them have hardly any furniture left up top, and what little there is, is higgledy-piggledy."

We'd reached the front door. From Madame's boat neck-line she withdrew a gold chain – I watched the outline of the front door key move sinuously up beneath the silky cloth of her dress to appear in the hollow of her neck. A little smile played around her carefully reddened lips and for a moment I imagined her lover nuzzling the bare cleft between her breasts where the key had rested. Before I could bite back the words, I said, "Mum tells me you have a lover."

I expected hysterics, histrionics, mum summarily dismissed from the sanctum of Shepherd's Fennel. On the contrary, Madame looked quietly delighted.

"Did she indeed? Dolly Littler is very naughty."

She unlocked the door and gently ushered me out into the chill autumn air.

***

Which set me a-thinking in a higgledy-piggledy fashion, on the train back to Victoria, of Steff and Rachel, Rachel and Jim, Susan and her married lover Caroline (and the dreaded daughter Angel Baby), and Susan and Jenny. Was 'all fair in love and war'? Then paring all my thoughts down to love – could that be helped, should it be denied if other people would be hurt?

I bumped along in the almost empty train carriage, my notebook open at a clean page waiting for something amusing and pithy to materialise. Nothing did. After two years all these random thoughts and soul-searching were so much dense shrubbery, concealing the question: "Where was Susan now?"

"Do you still miss Freddy?" Steff asked, twining her fingers around the stem of her wine glass and resting her chin quizzically on one wrist. By candlelight, she looked as young as when I'd first seen her in the Underground train on my way to visit mum in hospital. All the lines of pain and anxiety were smoothed away.

"Joan?" she prompted.

I was tempted to tell the truth; Steff would understand, but then again she'd turn it into something more serious. It wasn't easy making Steff laugh any more, she rarely saw the funny side. No – "I invented Freddy to make people like me. As part of a couple I'm attractive and amusing, an asset to any dinner party, but just Joan just isn't good enough" – wouldn't do.

I'd be forced to see a therapist, encouraged to read thick books in small print with copious footnotes, attend assertion classes. If I was asked out and about, it would be because 'Joan needs to know she's liked', rather than my infallible wit.

"We keep in touch," I said, "Every three or four months, there's a letter or a postcard. That woman has itchy feet – travels all over Europe. This was the last card I received – from the Camargue of all places."

I took a postcard from the small stack of Freddy postcards on the dresser and read out, " 'Flat beach with jetsam in the Gulf of Beauduc,' that's the picture on the front." I flipped the card over to show Steff a scene of a deserted beach with what looked like the skeleton of a buffalo in the foreground. I read on, "Joanie darling, for the first time in many weeks the sun is not moving along its glaring trail. An unusual stillness has fallen over steppes and marshes that is different from that of the preceding, heat-pulsating days. How you, with your deep love of the sea, would appreciate the isolated beauty of this place. Always true, Freddy."

"Sounds rather Graham Greenish," Steff said.

"Do you think so? Freddy has rather a way with words."

"When will you see her again?"

"We've made a pact. More apple charlotte?"

"I couldn't, really."

"At eleven a.m., New Year's Day, the year 2000, we're going to meet on the steps of the Taj Mahal. Freddy will have already been in Agra for a couple of weeks, so she'll be able to show me around."

"But Joan, won't it be rather crowded on that particular day? How can you be sure of spotting each other?"

I quelled a sigh. The more decent and sensitive someone was, the more difficult it was for a lie to go unchallenged, even if it was in the nicest, most caring way. Now, Susan would have let my complete 'Freddy abroad' rigmarole pass, half believing, half not believing, and enjoyed trying to catch me out. I looked into Steff's honest, troubled eyes and said, "We're wearing very tall orange pixie hats – Freddy's idea. Just a bit of fun, but it should do the trick."

Immediately Steff looked relieved and said, "I like the sound of Freddy."

I smiled, "We're not an 'item', any more, but we're still very close."

The Freddy postcards and letters had been surprisingly easy to manage. Three times a year Mrs Botolph visited Europe, usually in a group of well-off, Shoreham and environs, widowed ladies. I'd told her I had my sights set on becoming a philatelist during my declining years, but I'd like to make an early start to see how I got on, whether it was really the hobby for me.

"I'd have liked to collect foreign stamps," mum had said wistfully.

"I can't organise foreign stamps for all and sundry."

"Just do mine then, Mrs Botolph – any duplicates I'll steam off and give to mum."

Mrs Botolph would send me a postcard, blank all but my

name and address, from wherever she went. Some she spoilt. She couldn't always resist writing, "Don't forget the *Telegraph* Jumbo Crossword for your mother," or, "Home on the 10th, ring the milkman," but most got through. I also issued her with several packs of sealed and addressed airmail envelopes. She grumbled that it made more work, couldn't I be satisfied with postcards, but I could see she was quite cheerful to be supporting Dolly's feckless daughter in a proper hobby.

I was now adept at reproducing Mrs B's handwriting to match my name and address. I enjoyed writing the Freddy cards and letters. I always carried one with me when I went out to dinner just in case I was asked, "Anything fresh from Freddy?" Sometimes I overdid the prose. Once Sash said with a bemused smile, "Freddy has a fine sense of the ridiculous."

"In what way?" I'd asked with a fixed, nervous smile.

"The bit about meeting that party from the colony of bee-eaters in the Rhône delta."

"Oh yes, that was very amusing. Freddy meets all sorts."

Later at home, I'd looked up bee-eaters in the dictionary: "Any of various insectivorous birds of the Old World tropics and subtropics." Write: Joan must be more vigilant, twenty times.

I'd built a fire for the first time that autumn; the sitting room looked warm and inviting lit by the flames. We sat together on the sofa inhaling the pleasing scent of logs burning and the less pleasing smell of old cat, emanating from Edith who lay stretched out on the rug, as close to the heat as possible without being cremated.

It was comfortable and easy sitting with Steff. Although we'd become good friends again, this was the first time she'd been to dinner when there'd been no other guests.

In the orange flickering light I watched her staring dreamily into the flames. I liked her face – fine-boned, dark intelligent eyes that usually looked unhappy or ill at ease. Not that evening, at that moment. We finished our glasses of wine; she looked up and met my gaze.

"A brandy?" I said, "I could open another bottle…"

She hesitated, smiling, "No. I should be going soon."

"You could stay… There's this settee or I can change the sheets on Jenny's bed," I added hurriedly.

She put her wine glass down on the hearth, then turned back to me. Very gently, she began to stroke my cheek, then sliding her hand into my hair, she drew my face to hers. Her lips were soft and warm, tasting of wine. I realised then how desperate I was for love and warmth and proximity; a soft body pressed into mine and yet… I heard the clock ticking, a log shifted in the fire… we drew apart.

"I don't think I can, Joan," Steff said, "I'm sorry."

I laughed shakily, "That's OK. I could have but it wouldn't have been the same."

"The same as Freddy?" she probed gently.

"The same as Susan," and I began to cry. Nothing noisy, perhaps the odd snuffle, just tears flowing quietly down my cheeks in a curtain of unstoppable water.

SEVENTEEN
1999
It's my party

I was forty-six and I knew now, I'd never be slim again. Over the years, unnoticed and unchallenged, my bones had grown bigger. These days there was something of the shire horse about me – I hoped something endearing.

"But not today, Joan. You have minimised your excesses. You have a figure of sorts. You look well groomed and expensive."

I wore a pair of wide chenille trousers in a deep burgundy shade.

"With your height you can get away with harem trousers," the assistant had said, flicking through the rails, a cigarette balanced on her bottom lip, "Team them with this."

I hadn't been as impressed with the 'this': a hip-length tunic in a moist material, a spray of diamanté cascading from a rhinestone star on one shoulder. I turned sideways and smoothed the tunic over my stomach, "Not bad, Joan, if you remember to only ever breathe in."

I jingled the two gold-plated bracelets I'd bought earlier in the week from Argos. Yes, as an ensemble, I certainly didn't look like Joan Littler.

Downstairs the doorbell rang yet again. I heard faintly familiar voices, loud at first, then merging into the hum of conversation coming up from the room beneath me.

"Whatever are you doing?" Steff was peering through the gaps between the banisters.

"Almost ready. What do you think?"

She came slowly into the bedroom, frowning.

"It's an ensemble," I said weakly.

"Where did you get it?"

I opened my mouth to say, "Selfridges," and said, "Dalston."

"I thought so. That top's awful. The trousers aren't too bad."

"What about the bracelets?"

"No comment. Put this on," she pulled a jumper out of my wardrobe, "You always look nice in this."

"I wanted to look a bit more than 'nice'."

Steff sighed but with a patient smile, "Joan, accept that you're out of touch when it comes to clothes, what you've got on is the sort of outfit sad bad singers wear on cheap cruise ships."

"How would you know?"

"Trust me."

I put the jumper on and added my lucky dolphin, pushed up my sleeves so my bracelets were visible and followed Steff. On the bottom stair a girl of about ten was sitting. She looked up at me with a good-natured scowl: "Mrs Botolph said to say, 'Get a move on.' "

"Thank you Ruth, what do you think of these trousers?"

"They're old-fashioned. I like skin-tight clothes."

"Do you indeed?" I tweaked her nose in passing, "Girls of your age should wear smocks and aprons."

"What's a smock?"

The sitting room door was flung open and there was Mrs Botolph, sailing towards me, a picture in shocking pink grosgrain. (Heavy ribbed silk or rayon fabric – nine letters.)

"Happy birthday Joan, and well done. Your mother would have been proud of you... at long last." For a moment her lower lip trembled and she dabbed at her eye with a serviette.

I kissed her powdery cheek awkwardly, "Thank you, Mrs Botolph."

"Joan, we did enjoy it... so true to life... very funny. I said to Gran, I don't remember Joan being funny." Gemma appeared out of Mrs B's large shadow like a small pregnant tug-boat. Tug-boat simile aside, she looked marvellous. Something had obviously gone very right for her – her eyes sparkled and her skin was her grandmother's favourite colours: pink and cream.

"Of course, Dolly was very dry. That's her mother," Mrs Botolph informed several people who'd spilled out into the hall.

"My mother," I mouthed.

"We can't wait for the next episode. We're videoing it," Gemma said.

"Thank you," I said, and "Congratulations to you and..."

Gemma flushed and wriggled attractively. Mrs Botolph laid a jewelled hand on my arm. "Before you jump to any conclusions, Joan..."

"I wasn't."

"Oh, I know how you writer johnnies work, something perfectly innocent gets distorted into an X-rated film."

"I don't think..."

"There's no particular father involved, it could be a number of men."

"Good heavens," I murmured.

"Oh yes, think on. You're not the only one can get up to this promiscuous lark."

Gemma fluttered her eyelids in a bold and provocative manner and said, "I've had to grasp what life offered me, Joan."

"Don't respond," Steff hissed behind me, her knuckle pressed firmly against my spine, pushing me forward into the crowded room.

It was a birthday-cum-moving-house party – Steff's idea. It had also been Steff's idea for me to sell the house and buy a two-bedroomed flat with a smaller garden.

"With the money you make, you can afford to write full-time. No more gardening, no more lodgers."

I wasn't moving far – I couldn't leave Stoke Newington. I loved the pubs, the cheap restaurants and Turkish caffs, the myriad assortment of shops, and of course Woolworths, where no one stopped you from helping yourself to a couple of pick-n-mix to chew while wandering around the store, or standing lost in thought before a display of reasonably priced kitchenware.

"An unbeatable stock of Pyrex," I'd advised Jenny, when she'd finally set off for pastures revisited in Islington – she and Penny were negotiating an open relationship.

"Pyrex shrieks poverty," she'd said, shuddering. "I'll be glad to see the back of your Pyrex and your home-grown vegetables."

Penny had my deepest sympathy.

Life for some had turned full circle; for Steff and Rachel, not quite. Rachel had relinquished Jim and normality in Welwyn Garden City and was living with Ruth, no longer Persephone, in a commune in Haggerston. She had become an avowed celibate and was writing a reference book called *Kill Agamemnon*. I kept clear of Rachel, would never like or trust her.

"She's been a good mother to Ruth," Steff said, "Time to let bygones be bygones – you didn't used to take life so seriously."

Which was why she arranged my first ever birthday party.

I was more solemn. I saw it even in my relationship with Edith. We could sit for hours, not so much as a glance exchanged, contemplating our own thoughts.

My life chugged along fairly contentedly. I'd given up trying to be a stand-up comedienne; found I much preferred writing about humorous situations than trying to explain them aloud. I enjoyed sitting at my desk, musing between cups of tea and getting paid, sometimes, for a job that bore no resemblance to any work I'd done before. I was almost happy. For the first time ever I felt confident and fulfilled; a rounded Joan when once I'd needed someone else to make me whole.

Which didn't mean I wasn't lonely – I still hung on to my daydreams.

Steff had been thorough. She'd invited almost anyone I'd ever met over the last twenty-five years with the exception of Sandy Banks and her mother.

"They live in Edinburgh now. Sandy said they had no time for London – the air's cleaner where they are and she'd almost halved her dry-cleaning bill."

"You're joking, Steff, did you really speak her?"

"Really. Are you disappointed?"

"I'd have liked to see how she'd weathered, and Leila."

Nurse Duggan came, however – now Mrs Ronald Lewis (her third husband). They'd taken a weekend break in London so she could look in.

"We're going on to see *Phantom*, so we can only stop an hour or so. Sorry about your mum. I can't believe she lived that long. A wonderful, funny woman."

I smiled and nodded. Mum's death was too recent; I was

still unable to articulate the simplest sentence about her. Nurse Duggan, as she will always be to me, understood and changed the subject.

"We've both put the weight on. It's my breasts and buttocks. I can see it's breasts with you as well. Life's a funny old game – you always get too little or too much. What do you think, Ronald?"

Ronald shrugged and tugged a loop of grey hair over his eyes. I responded with the awkward half-curtsey I reduced myself to in moments of embarrassment, and made for the open door where I could see Penny squatting down by the fish pond. She was tickling one of the goldfish with a stalk of lavender.

"Will you take them with you when you go?" she asked without looking up.

"No. They're fixtures and fittings. Are you OK, out here on your own?"

"I'm used to it."

"Are you and Jenny...?"

"Susan's back."

"Oh," I said.

She shrugged, "I'm not worried. It's all over as far as the wonderful Susan's concerned, only it's depressing watching Jenny trotting after her still, like a pet dog."

"Is Susan on her own?" I asked.

"Who cares apart from Jenny? Anyway, Susan, for all her apparent charm, never did say much about herself, did she? I suppose that was her attraction."

"I know Jenny's very fond of you," I said gently.

"Is she? I hadn't noticed. Unfortunately I'm more than very fond of her. I can't be like you, Joan, holding yourself aloof from the battle."

"I didn't know I did."

"Of course you do. It doesn't go unnoticed. We're not all mugs. You refuse to get involved. Poor old Freddy must have got tired waiting for you to make a commitment. What are you holding out for – the love of your life to turn up, while the rest of us make do with compromise?"

"That's unfair."

"Is it? I don't care. I don't feel fair." She stood up and stretched, "God, my joints ache. I must be getting old."

She walked away towards the fruit trees at the bottom of the garden, her head bent but her shoulders very straight.

Susan was back. She sat on mum's threadbare ottoman, holding court in the bay window; impeccable as ever in a grey collarless shirt and dark trousers.

"What made you ask her?" I said to Steff.

She smiled impishly, "Curiosity. I wanted to see your famous Susan. She doesn't seem half as likeable as Freddy."

"You've never met Freddy."

"I feel I know her, from her cards and letters. Freddy's constant. I think that's a very precious attribute."

"Freddy will have to suffer a boating fatality in the Red Sea at some point," I thought sourly.

***

All the while observing Susan, I engaged in several earnest conversations about house prices in the South East and estate agents' fees. Each time she tried to catch my eye, I smiled with rapt enchantment and leant forward to better catch the pearls of wisdom dropping from the lips of whoever I was talking to. Inside, I was willing Susan to quit her place in my bay window, leave behind the puling Jenny in her various layers of cerise and navy chiffon and do something authoritative with my elbows.

"That one fancies herself a flower fairy." Mrs Botolph's bulk blocked me out of Susan's vision. "I'd say a fuchsia. Is that Susan? Your mother would have a fit. I hope you're not still smitten with her. She's a bad 'un."

"That's terribly fascinating, Mrs Botolph, but you must excuse me, I've hardly touched the champagne."

On cue, a small woman in a smart black dress materialised bearing a tray of champagne. I blinked. Was Steff mad? Joan Littler couldn't afford maids, nor champagne in this quantity.

"Hold on," I said as she turned away. If I was paying then I was drinking. I downed one flute and helped myself to another.

"That's better," I said to nobody in particular.

I edged Jenny aside with the toe of my boot, "Penny's looking for you in the garden," I said.

"No point. I'm not in the garden."

"Well, could you go in the garden and find her?"

"Why should I?"

"Because I said so. It's my party and I'm not to be upset."

Jenny crouching on a footstool was no match for me. She looked yearningly for some hint from Susan. Susan shrugged.

"Well, don't let anyone take my footstool, I'll be right back," Jenny said and flounced away.

"Happy birthday," Susan said, moving to let me sit down next to her, "You're looking good."

"So are you."

But she wasn't. She looked tired, face a little puffy – then she smiled and said, "How's Freddy?"

"How's your extended family?"

"Touché. Caroline's in love with a lady poet half her age and Angel Baby's got her eye on a matador, provided he turns vegetarian and renounces all brutal sport."

"Where did you feature in this set-up?"

She looked serious for a moment, "After a while I didn't. Homesick and a bit directionless – not like me, was it? I gave up smoking which didn't help. Caro didn't like the smell in the house."

"Bit of a martinet," I said, and we both grinned. "Strict disciplinarian – eight letters."

"And Freddy? I thought she'd be here for your birthday, or have I just missed her?" Her eyes twinkled.

"She sent a card and a present," I waved my gold bracelets at her, "She's in Madagascar at the moment, in the capital – Antananarivo."

Susan raised her eyebrows, looked impressed, said, "In a pig's eye. Admit it, Joan, there never was a Freddy or a budgie called Barry."

"Bertie."

"You made it up. Got all your information from mum's encyclopedias and by the by, how is the ancient dragon-lady?"

"Dead," I said.

She closed her eyes. When she opened them again I could see, for just once, something had reached her.

"I'm sorry, Joan. When did it happen?"

"A few months ago."

She took a packet of cigarettes and a slim lighter from her shirt pocket.

"I thought you'd given them up."

"For emergencies only," she said. "Come into the garden Joan."

"Penny and Jenny are in the garden."

"No. Deirdre and Sash have them pinned down by the fireplace."

It was dusk – quite warm still. We walked together silently – a little awkward in each other's company.

"I am sorry," she said again.

"Yes," I said.

We traversed the lawn – that was how it seemed, Victorian and formal – Susan checking my roses for mildew as she had done all those years ago in mum's garden. She started humming quietly, 'Funny How Time Slips Away.'

"Who sang that, Joanie?"

"Georgie Fame or Ray Charles."

We stopped at the first apple tree. I waited for her to say something about all the windfalls rotting in the grass. She didn't.

"I've missed you," she said, "I could have coped with Spain if you'd been there. You... lighten the atmosphere."

"Thank you. What about Caroline?"

"You can't rekindle cold fires."

"Aren't we a cold fire?"

"We never gave the fire a chance to go out."

"And Jenny?"

"Jenny was keeping my hand in."

"Poor old Jenny."

"Jenny can take care of herself. Look Joan, this may not be the best time, but when did I ever let that stop me?" she paused.

"Go on."

"I've always missed you. For nearly twenty-five years there's been a gap in my life and her name was Joanie."

I looked at Susan, not quite a shadow among the trees – all I could see of her I loved dearly, all I heard of her I loved wryly. But it seemed impossible. Who would want a Joan who wasn't light and uncaring, a Joan being heavy; opening her mouth and saying, "Only Freddy calls me Joanie, and Susan, I am not going to beg you to tell me you love me, but missing me, having a gap in your life whose name is Joanie, won't do." I opened my mouth and said it.

I didn't wait for a response; any avowal of love, however bizarre, at that moment, would have rung false. I made my way through the house via the kitchen, muttering something about visiting Oddbins immediately. In the hall I grabbed my jacket from the pile over the banisters.

"Where are you going?" Ruth asked from her station on the third stair up.

"To the cinema," I said. "Tell Steff."

EIGHTEEN
The deeper things

I didn't have much time left and it was a job that had to be done. I put Susan out of my head. How many times over the years had I put Susan out of my head?

On the train I mused dismally on the responsibilities one assumes, once one takes on even the slightest burden of friendship – suddenly you weren't your own woman any more.

Nerves set in outside Shoreham Station. Bugger Mrs Botolph – she'd plagued me all my life – any low self-esteem I might have could be put down to her, mum and Mrs Scott, forever shutting doors against me so they could indulge in their grown-up confabs. I should go home immediately and refuse to speak to her if she telephoned.

"Contact my solicitors if there's a problem." Only... I didn't have a solicitor, and... when I'd felt lost and utterly alone after mum's funeral, she'd been, as they say, 'kindness itself'. For four days, I'd stayed in her guest bedroom, dragging myself out between sleep and depression to sit on her balcony wrapped in pink and primrose blankets. In a Botolph-like manner she'd fussed over me – her brusqueness rarely softening – a tough, no-nonsense kindness which helped me far more than mutual tears and sympathy.

We had talked about mum, cautiously at first; neither quite trusting the other. By the third day we were remembering events, things she'd said and done that had made us both laugh.

Mrs Botolph never cried. I realised she only ever dabbed at her eyes – that was her outward show of grief – the rest she kept inside.

"Those foreign classics – what did you make of mum beginning to read them?" I asked eventually. "Was it because she knew she was dying – getting serious at last?"

She'd considered the view from the balcony, as if it might hold some answer, for several minutes. I'd thought what a fine old ship's figurehead she'd have made, providing there was a large enough piece of wood available to carve her from.

"I've given some thought to that myself," she said at last, "because I can't deny my feelings were hurt at the time. Those puzzles were our point of reference – had been for donkey's years. I never said anything, but I did feel excluded."

"It wasn't as if she could get through them all – if I started now, I doubt I'd get through all the foreign classics in my lifetime."

"That's not the only reason one reads books, is it, Joan?" she queried mildly. "I think we have to accept, there are areas where we're all unfathomable. That's certainly been true of you, Joan," she said sourly, forgetting for a moment we were both recuperating under a flag of truce. "Your mother was multi-faceted – I don't think we always appreciated that."

A few days later she'd telephoned me at home.

"I've been doing some thinking and I've come to a conclusion. It was much better for Dolly to die halfway through *Doctor Zhivago* than slumped over an unfinished *News of the World* crossword. We must remember her as still avid, Joan. Hungry for life – four letters."

Mrs Botolph was in her dressing gown when I arrived: ankle-length, turquoise velour, which made a large bright splash against her ice-cream tinted walls and carpets.

"I'm having my cup of tea on the balcony," she said, unsurprised at finding me unannounced in her hallway at ten o'clock in the morning, "I'm afraid you've just missed Gemma, she's gone with a man-friend to her Natural Childbirthing class."

"How is she? She looked positively radiant at my party," I gushed, handing her an off-white cyclamen.

She sniffed the air, didn't quite paw the ground with her fluffy slipper; a Joan bearing gifts and compliments meant something was very wrong.

"Gemma's being carefully monitored," she said cautiously, "Coffee or tea?"

It was crowded on the balcony. Apart from a new circular wrought-iron table, matching chairs with floral cushions which in turn matched the sunbed upholstery, there was a baby buggy wrapped in clear plastic. From the hanging baskets of late-flowering geraniums, two wooden mobiles swung – a flight of mallard geese and a flight of pink pigs, the pigs catching me at brow level as I picked my way towards a chair.

I sat facing the sea – velour dressing gown coloured, with a line of green on the horizon.

"So Joan, what has to be said face to face that can't be said on the telephone?" She bustled on to the balcony with her tray.

"I see you still like buttered scones," I said lightly.

"The plot thickens," she muttered.

While she poured the tea, I marshalled my thoughts. It was going to be difficult. I watched Mrs Botolph's hands, stirring teabags, adding hot water, spooning sugar. Beautiful hands, a sprinkling of age spots that could pass for freckles in summer; her nails were manicured and varnished a frosted magenta. As always, she wore her glittering costume jewellery. I imagined her reaching for her rings and bracelets automatically every morning, before she reached for her spectacles or slippers.

Her hands shook. Not from nerves. That woman has no nerves. The invincible Mrs Botolph was growing frail.

"Spit it out. What have you done now?"

"I think it's going to be a case of, 'Joan, you never fail to disappoint me.' "

"Well, don't disappoint me by not disappointing me."

I took a deep breath – reached for a scone – reconsidered

and clasped my hands together.

"The fact of the matter is... in next week's episode you become a lesbian."

I waited for a pin to drop, a sharp intake of breath – all I heard was the distant murmur of the sea which may have been the murmur of the traffic on the coast road – I was too much an inveterate Londoner to differentiate. Mrs Botolph rearranged the knitted shepherdess over the teapot before responding.

"What about your mother and Mrs Scott? Are we to be a coven of lesbians?" Her expression was unreadable.

"I kept their proclivities –" she raised a pencilled eyebrow "– rather vague. Basically, you... Mrs Dunbarton falls in love with mum."

"Dottie Fisher."

"Yes. Dottie does reciprocate Mrs Dunbarton's feeling but any sex is only intimated."

"Intimate?"

"No. Intimated. You know – implied." I nearly added, "Seven letters."

"And will there be nudity?" Mrs Botolph's strong voice wavered uncertainly.

"Definitely no nudity. It's a comedy – loving, humorous relationships, set when you were all youngish women."

"A time you know nothing about."

Mrs Botolph sipped her tea, eyelids lowered. Mum had been transparent, or so I'd thought until just before she died; Mrs Botolph's emotions were harder to read.

Finally she put down her cup and looked directly at me.

"It isn't that I'm angry, Joan," for a moment she looked perplexed as if searching for a way to express herself in a foreign language, "although it would be easy to be deeply offended – you haven't been settling old scores, have you?"

I shook my head vehemently.

"And you haven't made fools of us all?"

Again I shook my head.

"I suppose I have to trust your judgement, but it better be good, Joan."

TAPE 5

Q: And was it good, Joan?

Joan: Yes, I think so. I had a letter from her, and I quote, "You have my cautious approval, subject to seeing the remaining four episodes. In the absence of your dear mother, I feel it falls to me to say, you'll sail close to the wind once too often. Read, learn and digest. Gemma has given birth to a seven-pound daughter. A possible name is still under discussion: 'Joan' has been mooted.

Q: So, creatively it's all systems go, but what of the future? Will you and Freddy bond on the steps of the Taj Mahal?

Joan: I fear a fatal fall for Freddy. I shall wear black and nurse a hidden grief which will mean friends will make allowances for me and interviewers treat me kindly.

Q: Until this interview is broadcast in the autumn.

Joan: I'm used to periods of isolation.

Q: Finally, Susan. Is she, was she the love of your life? The truly madly deeply woman?

Joan: What do you think?

NINETEEN
Mrs Botolph shows uncanny foresight

I walked out into Langham Place. I'd been excited at the prospect of a radio interview, now I felt a little flat – a little lonely. It was a Tuesday and nothing much happened in my life on Tuesdays. The evenings were generally spent ironing, then falling asleep on the settee having only read a page or two of my book. Steff had come over that morning to help me finish packing in a non-obtrusive manner to avoid alerting Edith to the forthcoming move, but she'd be gone by the time I reached home – Tuesday was her evening with Ruth.

The sun was sinking behind the buildings, leaving a warm glow to the sky and several benevolent clouds edged with gold. I watched a plane fly overhead, the last rays of the sun reflected on its wings. Reluctantly, I turned in the direction of the Euston Road. A brisk walk might do me good. Just as far as King's Cross station, then a rough and tumble to get on board the crowded 73 bus – small changes, unlooked-for exertion, often set the adrenalin running, turned my mood around.

I didn't notice the silver-grey Ford parked on double

yellow lines, hazard lights flashing. I passed it by, deep in thought.

"Joan," Susan shouted.

I stopped. Fighting back a smile, I walked over to the car.

"What happened to the Land Rover?" I asked coolly.

She slapped the outside of the car door fondly, as if it were the glossy rump of a beloved horse. "No good for town driving, gone back to my old true love. Hop in."

"Actually, I'd rather walk, it's such a glorious evening." I smiled politely, affectedly – austerely? I was a Victorian heroine putting down an importune suitor. Then it struck me: "How did you know where I was?"

I didn't quite like the look of her smile, more of a jubilant grin than a smile.

"Your friend Steff told me you were here being interviewed."

"Steff?"

"I went to your house."

"Oh," I said, "Well, it was kind of you to come all this way, but I think I'd rather…"

"She was in the middle of packing, so I answered the telephone. It was dear old Ma Botolph to say her friend Maisie hadn't been able to post the Guatemalan postcards. I couldn't help it, Joan, I've a naturally enquiring mind, I put two and two together and sometimes get the right answer. Just a shot in the dark but I asked her by whom and when the card had been sent from Madagascar."

"And?" I said coldly.

"She said she'd posted it herself, that Joan wanted it by

her birthday, something to do with the postmark and the end of the century. Madagascar wasn't all it was cracked up to be and she wouldn't be going again." Susan was laughing now, "Joan, you're not going to tell me that Mrs Botolph's really Fearless Freddy, are you?"

"The woman's mad, absolutely raving mad," I said.

"That's exactly what Steff said, when I told her. She has complete faith in the Freddy saga."

That was the moment when I lost my nerve, the moment when all the people who'd ever asked me "How's Freddy?" began to parade in front of me, every one of them wearing untarnished haloes, their affectionate smiles for good old Joan fading into hurt bewilderment. If Susan didn't get there first, by autumn – a few short months away – everyone would know. What had I done? I felt cold with fear. Susan was still smiling up at me, waiting for some amusing riposte.

"Susan," I wailed, "I shall be in such trouble. Everyone will hate me – they'll know I've lied and lied. I'll have to change my name, leave England – the newspapers will pick it up – I'll look a complete fool."

"The newspapers? Nobody's ever heard of you. Get in the car," she said.

I got in the car. She put on a Millie Jackson CD, full of sad songs about doing wrong and being done wrong to, while I counted those who'd shrug their shoulders and say, "Why of course we knew Joan Littler lied, it's never really mattered to us."

There was mum, who couldn't help.

Mrs Botolph, who wouldn't help...

And Susan.

"I don't know why you're so worried, nobody need ever know – I won't tell anyone – I half knew anyway," Susan said.

"I told Pat," I said in a deadly voice.

"Pat?"

"Pat Cameron. The interviewer."

"Why?"

"I don't know. At the time it didn't seem to matter – it was still in the distant future, still amusing. But you knowing, Steff knowing but not believing, suddenly it all seems..." I was lost for words.

"Joan – you walk into the pub, toss your head the way you do when you're about to make a totally untrue statement..."

"Do I?"

"Of course you do. Then that deep, warm chuckle of yours, and say: 'I'm afraid the truth lies somewhere in the middle,' squeeze my arm, stroke my hair, then enigmatically add, 'Only Susan knows what really happened with Freddy, and her lips are sealed.' "

"And you'll back me up?"

"Yes."

"What if you're not there?"

"You better make sure I am there." She reached for the ignition, "There's a traffic warden heading our way, so I'l make this brief."

Hand still on the ignition, she turned to me, no smiles,

no twinkles – a serious Susan I couldn't remember seeing before.

"For what words are worth, Joan… When you were twenty-three I liked you a lot; going on fifty – I love you. I've never said that before – not to Caroline or any woman. I've felt other emotions, strong emotions, but not love. You're under my skin, and I'd rather you weren't. Take it or leave it, Joan – I'll drop you home whatever you decide."

I thought, "This can't be true. Fairy-tale endings don't happen to the Joan Littlers of this world," and yet I believed her.

The car moved out into the traffic. I buckled my seat belt and relaxed as we headed towards what was left of the sunset.

"You can call me Joanie," I said softly.

Emerald Budgies
Lee Maxwell

"Great flocks of emerald budgies are flying through your brain..."

Ruth is in a state. The kind of state where you might put a hedgehog under the wheel before reversing, or pull on rubber underwear before running drugs to a colleague.

Things aren't going to get any better till the memory she's been avoiding floods back into her mind – and after that, they'll get a lot worse.

Lee Maxwell's first novel is a darkly comic tale of disintegration, betrayal and revenge.

"Great energy – so much chaos – and I laughed out loud a lot too. This is a strange way to describe it but Emerald Budgies is really charming."
Emily Perkins

Published late June 2000   £8.95   ISBN 1-873741-44-8

DIVA Books are available from all good bookshops, or by mail order on 020 8340 8644 (international: +44 20 8340 8644) quoting the following codes: Needle Point DVB421, The Comedienne DVB43X, Emerald Budgies DVB 448. Subscribe to DIVA magazine for £24 (UK rate, one year, 12 issues).